INNOCENT
TARGET

REDEMPTION HARBOR SERIES

Katie Reus

Cover art: Jaycee of Sweet 'N Spicy Designs
Editor: Julia Ganis
Author website: http://www.katiereus.com

Publisher's Note: This is a work of fiction. Names, characters, places, and incidents are either the products of the author's imagination or used fictitiously, and any resemblance to actual persons, living or dead, or business establishments, organizations or locales is completely coincidental.

Innocent Target/Katie Reus. -- 1st ed.
KR Press, LLC

ISBN-13: 9781635560374
ISBN-10: 1635560373

eISBN: 9781635560367

For my sister.

Praise for the novels of Katie Reus

"Exciting in more ways than one, well-paced and smoothly written, I'd recommend *A Covert Affair* to any romantic suspense reader."
—Harlequin Junkie

"Sexy military romantic suspense." —USA Today

"I could not put this book down. . . . Let me be clear that I am not saying that this was a good book *for* a paranormal genre; it was an excellent romance read, *period*." —All About Romance

"Reus strikes just the right balance of steamy sexual tension and nail-biting action....This romantic thriller reliably hits every note that fans of the genre will expect." —*Publishers Weekly*

"Prepare yourself for the start of a great new series! . . . I'm excited about reading more about this great group of characters."
—Fresh Fiction

"Wow! This powerful, passionate hero sizzles with sheer deliciousness. I loved every sexy twist of this fun & exhilarating tale. Katie Reus delivers!" —Carolyn Crane, RITA award winning author

"A sexy, well-crafted paranormal romance that succeeds with smart characters and creative world building."—Kirkus Reviews

"*Mating Instinct*'s romance is taut and passionate . . . Katie Reus's newest installment in her Moon Shifter series will leave readers breathless!"
—Stephanie Tyler, *New York Times* bestselling author

CHAPTER ONE

—Some days should come with a warning label.—

Hadley adjusted her backpack as she reached the edge of the dark parking lot where she'd parked her car. Normally this lot was fully lit up this time of night. The college was intense about security.

Frowning, she scanned the surrounding grassy areas, which were now covered in shadows from the giant oak trees. In the daytime, this place was gorgeous and teeming with life. Now it was creepy. Really wishing that Cindy, her classmate, had been in class tonight to walk with her like they normally did, she pulled out her cell phone instead. Using her phone's flashlight app, she held it up as she hurried across the parking lot.

She could see the outline of a couple cars, including her own, but only because she knew where she'd parked it. Directly under one of the lights.

Which was currently out.

Maybe there had been a power outage on part of the campus? Seemed weird, since there hadn't been a storm, but who knew. She was new to the college and living in South Carolina. Redemption Harbor had a great vet school, which was a huge part of why she was here. But she'd really wanted to get to know her new family. Applying for school here before she'd met her half-brother had been a risk, but she'd gone for it because of the stellar program. She'd grown up knowing who her father and half-brother were, but until a couple months ago they hadn't even known she'd existed.

For so long she'd stayed away from them because of her mom's lies. Now she knew and loved her father and half-brother. They were overprotective and could sometimes be overbearing, but she was learning how to create boundaries and make them stick. Because holy crap, those men were like big bulldogs who seemed to think she was made of spun glass. And her brother's friends—male and female—were just as protective.

Picking up her pace, she hurried toward her red car. As a woman, she'd learned not to put herself in risky situations from a young age. It was like breathing; it was simply what you did. So right now she was pissed off on principle that all the lights in this parking lot were off and she didn't have a friend to walk with.

And she was also kicking herself for not putting the pepper spray her brother had given her in her backpack. No excuse for that.

As she reached her car she pressed the key fob and slipped her backpack off. Just as she reached for the door handle, two rough hands grabbed her shoulders from behind and slammed her against the car.

Crying out, she threw a hand up to brace herself but the side of her head hit the top of her car. Pain ricocheted through her skull, jarring her.

Before she even had time to react or fight back, her attacker wrapped an arm around her throat.

Adrenaline jagged through her, sharp and cutting. *No. Oh God, no!* She couldn't pass out. Then he could do whatever he wanted, even transport her from here, or kill her.

No!

Hadley reared back with an elbow and jabbed the guy in his stomach but he didn't even react.

He didn't say anything at all, which made it somehow worse. She felt as if she was dying. A thump sounded as she kicked out, accidentally slamming her foot into her car. More pain registered but she ignored it as she tried to stay awake.

Tears stung her eyes as she struggled and thrashed, even as he tightened his grip on her throat. Everything was getting fuzzy, and in the back of her mind she knew that she was going to pass out soon. She tried to scream but nothing would come out as he kept up the pressure on her windpipe.

Frantic, she lifted her legs and used her feet to shove off her car, propelling them backward. He stumbled once.

Abruptly his hold loosened and she fell to the concrete pavement. Her palms slammed against the ground even as she heard the male grunting.

Run. Hide. Now.

Turning and lifting her hands to shield herself from the attack she expected she...froze. They weren't alone anymore. Thanks to muted moonlight she could make out two men fighting in the dark but they were both shadowy figures.

One had a mask and the other had a big beard.

What was happening? Fear snaked through her even as she told herself to run. It held her immobile, however, as she watched the bearded guy slam his fist into the other masked man's face.

A crunching sound rent the air as bone broke.

The other man slumped and the one with the beard hauled the other guy up, tossing him over his shoulder as if he weighed nothing. Then he dumped him in the trunk of a nearby car.

The guy didn't even look her way, just slammed the trunk shut, slid into the driver's seat and took off without turning on the headlights.

Hadley shoved up, but stood there, shaking.

What...had just happened?

She heard a rushing sound as she remained there in the darkness and realized it was blood pulsing in her ears.

A popping sound in the distance, like a car back-firing, snapped her back to life. Scrambling, she reached for her fallen backpack and phone. Fighting back tears, she jumped in her car and locked it. When she looked at her phone she realized barely two

minutes had passed since she'd been attacked. Everything had happened so quickly, time seeming to stretch
out for an eternity. And she was trembling so bad she felt
as if she'd come apart at the seams.

She had to do something. Her brain refused to func-
tion for a long moment and she realized she needed to
call campus police. Both her brother and dad were out of
town so she would call them later. And she needed immediate help.

After a few tries, she managed to correctly put her
phone's code in and dial the number. Starting her car,
Hadley kicked it into drive even as a voice answered on
the other end.

"Redemption Harbor Campus Police, how may I help
you?"

"I n-need to report an assault on c-campus."

* * *

With a trembling hand, Hadley knocked on Mary
Grace's front door. She'd texted her friend earlier and
had been told that of course she could stop by. Hadley
should have just gone straight home after the attack, but
she didn't want to be alone right now. Admitting that,
even to herself, took effort.

Seconds later Mary Grace opened the door, a big
smile on her face. Almost immediately that smile mor-
phed into a frown.

Grasping Hadley's cold hands, she tugged her inside and shut the front door behind her. "What's wrong?" Mary Grace's dark hair was down around her face in soft waves, highlighting her café au lait skin and wide, dark eyes.

Because of the way she'd been raised, Hadley's instinct was to deny that there was anything going on, but Mary Grace was an observer by nature, as she had learned in the last couple months. Nothing got by the sharp oncologist.

Hadley swallowed hard. "It's, ah... Just..." She took a deep breath and started to tell her exactly what had happened just as Skye stepped into the foyer, her auburn hair pulled back into her trademark braid.

Crap. She hadn't realized the other woman was here. She'd known that Nova and possibly one of Mary Grace's sisters would be here but Skye was something else altogether. She was a little scary and kind of a badass. Admitting that an almost-mugging had scared Hadley made her feel stupid and weak in front of Skye. She'd been so unprepared during that attack. And she knew that she'd been damn lucky because she could have been... Yeah, no need to outline it in her head. Again. She'd been berating herself the entire drive over here.

"It's nothing," she muttered, hoping Mary Grace would let it go.

Mary Grace's frown was firmly in place as she wrapped an arm around her shoulders. They were about the same height and she resisted the urge to lay her head on Mary Grace's shoulder. From the time she was a kid she'd learned to pull back from emotional attachments, to not get too close and definitely not to overshare. That had started to change the last couple months, but old habits and all that. Plus she was still shaken by the attack.

"Come on, Nova's here too," Mary Grace said. "My sister couldn't make it so it's just us. And you're going to tell us what's going on."

Skye stiffened slightly, going into what Hadley thought of as battle mode. As if she was ready to start throat-punching anyone she deemed a threat. The woman could be intense. "What's wrong? Did someone hurt you?"

"No, sorta…yes," she sighed. Luckily she had on a turtleneck so they couldn't see the faint bruising on her throat. "I'll just tell everyone in the kitchen." Because she didn't want to tell the story more than once.

As she stepped inside the homey kitchen, she was greeted by a smiling Nova. "We didn't think you could make it tonight." The brunette bombshell was drinking a glass of red wine, her legs crossed as she leaned gracefully against the center island.

Skye picked up her bottle of water even as Mary Grace went to grab one for Hadley. "So what's up, half-pint?"

Some of the tension left her shoulders at the nickname. "Ah...something weird happened at school tonight. Or after." Quickly she launched into the near-mugging. Or...whatever her attacker had intended. For now, she was pretending he'd just wanted her wallet when she was pretty sure it was more than that. She'd been a woman, alone in a parking lot—he'd likely wanted to rape her. And possibly kill her. She knew that deep down. It was just difficult to think about.

All three women listened intently as she recounted everything from the first attacker, to the newcomer who took out her attacker, right up until she'd left the campus police office.

"How did they treat you at the office?" Skye demanded, her expression fierce.

"Ah, fine. They were nice. And they work with the locals... I guess it's sort of a combined thing. They're real cops, not like mall cops." That had made her feel better, since she'd given an official report. She gingerly touched her neck and hid a wince.

"What about security footage?"

"There was a glitch or something and for the last couple hours all footage on campus has been erased. Everything goes offsite though, so they said in a couple weeks they should have more. Might be able to see what actually happened. But I'm betting no since there were no lights in that lot."

"Was it just that lot?" Skye asked.

"No, there was an electric outage on the west side of the campus." Hadley was still unsure how that was possible and the cops hadn't seemed to know either.

"Huh."

"Don't start," Mary Grace murmured, giving Skye a hard look.

Skye lifted her palms up. "I didn't say anything."

"I can literally hear the wheels turning in that crazy head of yours. And you've got a look about you."

Skye snorted but simply shrugged. "Well...the mugging—which wasn't a mugging at all—was weird. And you're not even sure which guy, the bearded one or the masked one, was attacking you. My money is on the masked guy being your attacker, since he felt the need to cover his damn face, and the bearded one kicked his ass. But...that whole situation is weird. And don't even deny it," she snapped out, returning Mary Grace's hard look.

"I agree," Hadley said, sighing. "It was weird, but what the heck can I do about it? I'll park somewhere different once school starts back after spring break and make sure I always have a buddy with me."

"You can also start carrying pepper spray and maybe let Brooks hire you a bodyguard."

Hadley started to laugh but paused at Skye's set expression. "Please tell me you're joking."

"I am...mostly. Not about the pepper spray though. And I still don't like what happened. It's weird, and weird is never good."

"Sometimes weird is good," Nova murmured, her expression turning sly as she looked at Skye. Hadley had learned that Nova was often the one to break tension if there was any, and right now she was incredibly grateful for the light, almost teasing comment.

"Whatever, pervert," Skye growled.

Nova lifted a dark eyebrow. "I'm not the one who wears underwear with sexual sayings on my ass."

Hadley blinked once, then shook herself. "I've got this handled, you guys. Just...don't tell Brooks." She loved her brother but he was out of town with his fiancée right now and she didn't want to worry him or bring him back needlessly. Especially since nothing bad had actually happened.

"You're setting your security system every night?" Skye asked instead of actually agreeing that yes, she wouldn't tell Brooks.

"Leave the girl alone," Mary Grace said, sliding a glass of white wine in front of Hadley. "She's been through enough without adding an interrogation."

She wasn't normally a drinker, but after the night she'd had, she was making an exception. Because water wasn't going to cut it. "Thanks."

"I'm going to be looking into this," Skye said. "Fair warning. But I'll drop it for now since you're okay."

To her surprise, the others dropped the subject of what happened and they had a normal girls' night, something Hadley had never had before moving to Redemption Harbor. Her mom had been weirdly competitive with her, even with Hadley's own friends. Eventually she'd stopped bringing friends over.

Before she realized it, two hours had passed and Mercer, Mary Grace's husband, returned home, baby Mia cradled in his arms.

He smiled at all of them as he entered the kitchen, and Hadley had to refrain from reaching for the baby but only because she was sleeping.

"Gonna get her upstairs. Nice to see you guys," he said quietly to them.

"I'll be up in a bit. Oh, and Hadley is staying the night so make sure you wear clothes," Mary Grace added as her big husband stepped out of the room.

"Ah, what?" Hadley asked.

"Well you've had two glasses of wine and—"

"So I'm fine to drive home."

"Yes but Skye looks as if she's about ready to have a heart attack at the thought of you going home alone tonight so you'll stay here until she can ask Gage to hack the campus security system and get a look at your would-be mugger."

Hadley looked at the three women, all of whom didn't seem surprised by this suggestion. "You guys are being overprotective." She knew how to take care of herself and had been doing it for a long time.

Surprising her, Skye sidled up next to her and wrapped an arm around her shoulders. "Look, Brooks is out of town and he would lose his shit if he learned about what happened and then found out I did nothing to keep you safe."

"My house is safe." She knew her brother was co-founder of a security consulting company and yeah, she'd heard them talk about some gray area stuff before, but hacking her school's security seemed waaaayyyy over the top.

Skye simply squeezed Hadley's shoulders. "Come on. The Boy Scout can be so annoying when he's in a mood. Just humor us and stay here? You'll be doing me a favor."

"Oh my gosh, you're sneaky." She gently elbowed Skye but nodded even as she looked at Mary Grace, relieved that she wouldn't be alone after what had happened. "And so are you."

Nova just snorted into her wine and muttered, "You have no idea."

Even though Hadley thought they were being a teeny bit overprotective, she could actually admit that she didn't mind staying the night. What had happened at school had jarred her a lot deeper than she was ready to accept. And she wasn't sure how long it would take to put it behind her.

CHAPTER TWO

—Great things never come from comfort zones.—

With the sun shining on her face as she headed down the busy sidewalk to her favorite coffee shop, Hadley felt so much better this morning. It was amazing what some sleep could do. Still...she was a little off-kilter as if the sunlight and normal, happy people out and about were surreal. She hadn't slept well, and though she wasn't scared someone was going to jump out at her, she was still edgy.

After ordering her favorite drink—a mocha latte—she stepped outside and right into a wall of muscle. Her drink slipped from her hands, splashing all over the ground and a pair of scuffed boots.

"Oh my gosh, I'm so sorry." Horrified, she looked up into the clearest blue eyes she'd ever seen. "I'm..." *Um, words would be good. Now, please!*

"It's okay." The man's voice had a deep, sexy timbre she felt all the way to her toes. And other places. Well, that was new. She'd never been affected by a voice before, but this man was something else. He was maybe a little over six feet and his dark hair had auburn highlights that glinted in the sun. Freshly shaven and dressed casually, he was all sorts of sexy. "Let me buy you a new drink," he continued, stepping back so a couple could move past them.

That was when she realized they were standing in the middle of the doorway, blocking everyone. "Oh, ah, no, that's not necessary." Embarrassed, she bent to pick up her now empty cup and the top but he beat her to it and tossed them into the nearby recycle can.

"It's the least I can do." He looked at her with such intensity she swore she felt his warmth wrapping around her. Which was simply ridiculous.

"I wasn't watching where I was going."

"Fine, then you can buy me a drink," he continued, his lips kicking up in amusement.

Feeling her cheeks flush, she nodded and stepped back inside with him.

To her surprise, he ended up buying her drink and his—and getting her a chocolate muffin—in such a smooth way she hadn't even seen him pull out his cash.

"Thank you for this," she said once they stepped outside into the bright sunlight. Even if it was an un-usually cold spring, being around this man heated her right up.

Nodding, he glanced around in that hyperalert way she'd only ever seen her brother and his friends do. Maybe he'd been in the military? "It's no problem. Do you want to sit and talk with me or are you on your way somewhere?"

She loved the way he asked, giving her an easy out. Hadley rarely dated, and it wasn't as if he was asking her on one anyway. He was just asking her to join him for a few minutes and she really needed to stop overanalyzing things and say something. "Sure. I'm Hadley, by the way," she said as he pulled out one of the mesh wire chairs for her.

"Axel. Are you from around here?"

"I just started school here. Ah, vet school," she tacked on so he wouldn't think she was eighteen. At twenty-two, she knew she looked young, though this morning Mary Grace had let her borrow some clothes and Hadley could admit she felt sexy. Instead of her normal jeans and T-shirt, turtleneck or flannel button-up, she had on some sort of stretchy black pants with leather strips down the sides, little heeled boots and a formfitting sweater. She'd also borrowed a scarf for not only the cold, but to cover up the light bruising on her neck. "What about you?"

"I'm interviewing for a couple jobs so I'm in town for a week or so."

"Oh, what do you do?" She wasn't sure if it was rude to ask or not. She'd only ever dated guys from her last college so she'd known exactly what their "profession" was—student. And now, sitting in front of Axel she realized that the guys she'd dated were...boys in comparison. Given his build—tall, broad-shouldered but not bulky—she was pretty sure that he was built under his jeans, sweater and leather jacket.

He did that half-smile thing again that made butterflies take flight inside her. "Finance. Which means I crunch numbers and analyze stuff...it's pretty boring. So, vet school? What kind of background do you need for that?"

"I have a bachelor's in biology but there's not one specific degree you need. Having a science background certainly doesn't hurt though."

"What kind of vet degree do you want?" The man was so attentive, all his focus on her, and she'd seen a few women give him sidelong glances.

Not that she blamed them. Not one bit. "Well, you don't really get to pick. Like I can't say I want to go to school only for horses, but once I'm done I can have a focus in one area or another if I choose. I'm hoping to be an equine vet—a horse veterinarian."

"I've never been on a horse before. Or...even seen one in person, for that matter." Again with the toe-curling smile. There was just a hint of wicked in it.

Holy hell, he was making her panties melt, which was beyond ridiculous. At least it was taking her mind off yesterday. "They're not for everyone, but I love them." Her mom had allowed her one thing while growing up, horse-riding lessons. It had been pretty much the only nice thing her mom had ever done for her. Hadley knew it was because she'd liked to show Hadley off, as if she was a prize freaking pony herself, but she'd never cared since it allowed her to ride.

"Listen…I've got to run but I'd like to take you out sometime. Can I get your number?"

God, he was so straightforward, which she knew was good. She was simply used to being asked "wanna hang and grab a few beers" by guys. This felt different and she liked it. "Yes."

After she gave it to him, he texted her. "Now you've got mine too. I'll call you later today."

"Okay." She wasn't sure if he actually would call but she really hoped he would. She had so much going on right now, especially with starting a new school and program. But that didn't mean she couldn't have a little fun, right? She'd been so driven to succeed since…well, forever. Part of it was just her personality but part of it was because she'd been trying to earn her mother's approval. Something she'd only recognized recently. She wished she could think of something flirty or…anything else to say, but her mind was pretty much a blank as he stood and left.

She didn't even bother not trying to stare as he walked away because he seriously filled out those Levi's in a way that should be illegal. At least he gave her something to focus on after last night. Ugh. She needed to stop or she was going to send herself into a panic attack and hole up at home.

And on that note, she needed to get out of here too. She had errands to run, including heading out to the ranch to check on her favorite horse, Pirate. With her dad and brother out of town, they'd made it clear she had complete use of the estate anytime she wanted.

Which felt weird, considering how massive their estate was, but she really, really loved being able to go riding anytime she wanted. Plus it would give her some downtime, which she needed after last night.

* * *

Fuck.

Axel rubbed the back of his neck as he slid into the truck he'd rented. Hadley Lane was sexy as fuck. Adorable even, with that damn dimple and the way her cheeks flushed pink. She hadn't flirted with him at all, but she'd been sweet and open and... Hell.

He hadn't planned on this. Hadn't planned on her.

After he'd gotten a copy of a contract put out on her—sent by a friend who'd told him that this must be some sort of mistake and to check it out if he wanted—he'd done some digging. Once he'd realized she was related to Brooks Alexander he'd decided to visit Redemption Harbor in person.

Then he'd seen her in person yesterday. She was everything he wasn't.

And he found himself impossibly drawn to her. Like a moron. She wasn't for him. Not even close.

Yet...he was going to call her, spend time with her, but only to keep an eye on her. Because someone wanted her dead. And he hadn't figured out who yet. Whoever it was, was a dead man walking.

The only thing he knew for certain was that three hitters had been sent Hadley's information with instructions to kidnap her and bring her to a certain location unharmed. She was going to be used as leverage for something. Whatever it was wouldn't matter to the guys who'd been sent after her. They just wanted to get paid.

Now there were only two men he had to be on the lookout for because he'd taken care of one last night. That fucker had tried to kidnap her at school and had been smart enough to take out all the electricity in part of the college.

Axel had planted a tracker on her car earlier so he'd known where she'd be. Now...he should just contact Brooks and tell him what was going on.

When he saw the little dot on his phone moving, telling him that Hadley was heading somewhere else, he shelved the thought. He'd watch out for her now. She was so damn innocent and he couldn't stomach the thought of someone like her being hurt. He'd seen too many people hurt in his last profession and if he could look out for her, he would.

CHAPTER THREE

—Fact: you're an asshole.—

He stared at his laptop screen, as if that would some-how make the message he'd been waiting for ap-pear. He'd set up multiple anonymous email accounts and, with the help of an unsavory acquaintance, had reached out to men willing to do what he needed.

For a price, of course.

He was spending money he didn't have but he was a risk-taker. Sometimes his gambling paid off, and other times it didn't. Right now he desperately needed this plan to work. And kidnapping Hadley Lane was the way to get what he wanted quickest. It would serve two pur-poses.

Her rich father would do anything to get her back, and he planned to punish Douglas Alexander in more ways than one. That man would pay in blood eventually. But the old man wouldn't balk at a ransom request. Not for his precious daughter.

He wouldn't return her, however. Or maybe he would. Even if he did, she wouldn't be the same. He'd break her into a thousand pieces first. He'd decide that later, once he had the young, beautiful woman in his grasp. She was just his type too. Dark hair, sweet smile, all innocent and ripe for the picking.

And he was going to record everything for Douglas, make the old man watch what he did to her. It was nothing less than he deserved. Douglas had taken from him, mocked him as he did it, and now he would take from the billionaire.

For a while he'd considered Douglas's son, but Brooks was too hard to get to and he'd been in the Marines. A fucking sniper. No, going after him would be stupid. Those two had a poor relationship anyway. And Douglas's ex-wives had all been whores, none of whom the man seemed to care about at all. No leverage there.

But Hadley was sweet and new in his life. And by all accounts the man had "changed" and was trying to have a real relationship with her. A joke.

Nonetheless, this would still hurt Douglas, would cut him deep. Not only would he lose millions, he'd lose the daughter he'd never gotten to know.

Yes…he would have to kill her. Though he would wear a mask as he hurt her, cut her, raped her, he still would need her to die. Douglas would have to know that he'd never stood a chance at saving her. That no matter what he did, what he paid, his daughter would have died anyway.

Because he wanted to break Douglas too.

He refreshed his screen and nearly jumped when he saw a new message. He never actually sent the emails. He and the other man attached to this account simply signed into the email, started a new message, but never sent it. Just saved the messages as drafts. He had an email account set up like this with each man he'd hired.

Apparently it was the best way to communicate, per the acquaintance who'd given him the names of these men. He quickly scanned the message, frowned. Before responding he took a bump of coke to get settled.

Hitter 1: *You said you only hired a few of us.*

I did.

Hitter 1: *Saw the target out today with a known associate.*

Well, he certainly hadn't told the other men the names of who he'd hired. Just kept the contract small. His acquaintance had made that clear, that he could only hire a few hitters at a time and if they failed, only then could he expand his contract. Otherwise it would get too crowded and messy with too many people involved. And it would increase the chance of something leading back to him—or the job failing. It wasn't exactly strange that this guy saw someone in his field out with her. This guy should have been faster and gotten to her first—because no one got paid the full amount until she was brought in.

His frown deepened as he stared at the screen, ignoring his own reflection glinting off it. If Hadley was out with one of the men he'd hired, maybe the guy simply wanted to screw her first or drug her, bring her in easier.

Finally he responded. *What is the problem then?*

Hitter 1: *You said not to hurt her. Has that changed?*

Just bring her in alive and breathing. No broken bones.

If she was roughed up a little, he could deal with it. But he'd be the one to break her.

Hitter 1: *Okay.*

And that was that. He logged into the other accounts, hoping to find a message of success. Whoever H1 had seen the woman with might have already bagged her.

Adrenaline punched through him as he thought of what he'd do to her, of how Douglas would feel. But there were no emails, dousing part of the high from his last bump of coke.

Sighing, he closed down the windows and turned off his laptop. He could simply check from his phone later but he needed to get out of here.

Needed to meet up with friends, to be seen in public so he had an alibi later. And he was feeling lucky right now so it was time to hit the races, place a few bets.

Yeah, his luck was starting to turn around, he could feel it in his bones. Soon he'd get everything he deserved. And Douglas would regret the day he'd ever fucked with him.

CHAPTER FOUR

—Some days I like animals better than people.—

Axel knocked on Hadley's front door, still surprised by how small her house was. He knew it was, from his earlier covert visit to plant cameras around the exterior, but she was the daughter of Douglas Alexander. Axel had expected it to be much larger. Lavish, even. Not this cottage-style place in a quiet neighborhood with families. He'd set up a couple micro-cameras around her front yard and backyard too, covering all angles of her place so he could keep an eye on her.

He'd considered breaking into her place and adding a few inside, but he hadn't been willing to compromise her privacy like that. Not when he was able to monitor the exterior just fine. Even so, he hated that she wasn't somewhere safer, somewhere he could control the environment. Or at her family's ranch, which seemed almost impenetrable.

Tonight, at least, he hoped to change that. He wanted to get her away from her residence, an easily traceable place that anyone hired to kidnap her would target first. Her info was available and had been in the file he'd received regardless. But even if it hadn't been, tracking her down was child's play.

She opened the door wearing a little navy blue sweater dress and thigh-high boots, and it took a moment for his brain to start functioning again as he stared at her. In the pictures his contact had given him of her, she was always in jeans and T-shirts or sweaters—and looked amazing. With the mid-thigh dress hugging all her curves... Fuck him. He was so screwed. She was a decade younger than him and right about now he felt ancient.

Her cheeks flushed an adorable shade of pink as she smiled at him. "Hey."

"Hey, yourself. You look beautiful." He held out a small bag of the coffee beans he'd gotten from the same place they'd met.

Surprise flared in her dark eyes as she took the bag and smiled. When she smiled she had this one dimple that was absolutely adorable. No other word for it. "Thank you, I love this kind."

He'd debated getting her flowers, but had thought that felt wrong for some reason. Hell, this whole situation was wrong. He shouldn't be here. But he was, and damn it, he needed to get his head on straight. Axel couldn't afford to be distracted right now, not when he was trying to keep her safe.

Nodding once, he said, "I took a chance you would. Did you need a few more minutes before we head out?" He wasn't sure how current dating worked exactly since he hadn't been on one in... He couldn't remember. Which was pathetic.

"Ah, no... Did you want to come in for a drink before we go?"

He shook his head, even though he would like nothing more than to see her place—her bedroom specifically.

Still blushing, she grabbed her purse from a small foyer table as she set the coffee bag down. "Will you shut the door first? I need to set my alarm and can't do it if it's open."

At least she had a system in place. Nodding, he stepped inside with her, subtly inhaling her sweet vanilla and roses scent and trying not to stare too hard at her.

Once they were in his rental truck, he turned the music on low. "I have reservations at Bella Bella's but if you wanted, I could also cook for you at my rental place." Yeah, it was presumptuous but he wanted to get her in a location where she wasn't out in the open. "Please don't feel pressured to say yes. I just have a great view of the harbor." And more importantly, it would be difficult to attack her at his place.

No one would know where she was. Which was the whole point of tonight. Keep her safe. Hidden. Then... God, he needed to tell her someone wanted to hurt her.

"Ah...okay. Yeah, that sounds nice." Her voice was a little breathless and that damn blush was affecting him way more than he wanted to admit.

He was surprised she'd actually said yes. From her file, he knew she didn't date much, or at all it seemed. And he was annoyed she'd given him her address. Because she shouldn't be giving out her address to anyone, much less some guy she'd just met. But he couldn't very well chastise her for it without blowing his intent or sounding like a jackass.

"What's the address? I'm going to text a friend and let her know where I'll be." Then she snapped a picture of him—covertly, but not so much that he didn't realize what she'd done. Okay, so she was being cautious.

Damn. Maybe he'd been wrong. Good for her. He quickly rattled it off, glad she was taking safety precautions. Not that she needed to worry about him. He was dangerous, but not to her. Never to her. But no way in hell could she know that. Not when they'd just met. It eased some of the tension inside him. Damn it, he just needed to tell her what was going on, except...how did he tell her that someone had put out a contract on her head and wanted her kidnapped, without sounding crazy? Or admitting what he did for a living.

"So how did your job hunting thing go today?" she asked, crossing her legs slightly as she turned to face him more.

He lifted a shoulder. "Eh, interviews about finance and real estate. There's no way to make any of it sound exciting."

She laughed, the sound intoxicating. "Do you at least like what you do?"

Oh, that was a complicated answer. And even though he was lying about what he did for a living, he hadn't lied about his name. He hated the thought of lying to her in general. Which was new to him. And he wasn't sure how he felt about it. "Some days I do." Like today, because it had brought him to her.

"I understand that."

"So are you interning anywhere?"

"Not yet, but I hope to find something by this summer. Before I moved here I worked at a small veterinary clinic in an admin role for almost three years. But I got to sit in on a lot of things and it really enforced that I was making the right career decision."

"So why animals?" That was the kind of thing he couldn't read in a file. Some things he wanted her to tell him anyway. Because he wanted to know everything about this woman with the sweet smile and adorable dimple.

She snorted softly. "Will you judge me if I say because they're better than people most days?"

He barked out a surprised laugh at her honesty. "I understand." More than she could realize. Before his current profession, he'd worked for the FBI and he'd seen the worst in people in ways he didn't even want to think about. Especially from those who were supposed to be the good guys. "I'm surprised you don't have any pets. Unless you have one I didn't see?"

"Ah…I had a dog. Sassy. She died right before I moved here." There was a note of sadness in her voice.

"I'm sorry."

Hadley nodded once, her dark hair shifting slightly against her shoulders. "She was a rescue and her life hadn't been easy from what we could tell. When she was found she had a chain hanging from around her neck, poor thing. Honestly I'm surprised she lasted as long as she did, but at least I know her last few years were good. I got to bring her in to the clinic most days and she loved the attention." There was so much love and affection in her voice.

He'd never had a pet, not even as a kid. His mother had barely been able to take care of him, let alone an animal. "What kind of dog was she?" he asked as he turned into the gated community of the place he'd rented. The security here wouldn't stop a pro but it was one extra layer. And he didn't think they'd been followed. The men who'd been hired to take her were all loners so at least that eliminated the possibility of anyone working as a team.

"A shepherd-lab mix."

He nodded once as he pulled through the gates, keeping an eye on the rearview mirror. Nope. No one was behind him. And he hadn't noticed an obvious tail. When his phone buzzed he ignored it, even though he knew it had to be Isaac Murphy, the guy he had running info on Hadley's would-be kidnappers. He wasn't used to working like this, working to save someone in this way. Normally he simply took out assholes. And Isaac was a skilled hacker who helped him locate people.

"So…were you ever in the military?" Hadley asked as he pulled into the designated parking spot for the rental place.

Surprised by the question, he turned to face her. "Yes. Why?"

"You're just hyperaware in a way my ha…my brother is. And he was in the Marines."

He wondered if she'd been about to say half-brother. "I was too. Eight years."

"Oh wow. How…" Even in the dimness of the truck, there was enough outside illumination from the moon and other lights at the complex that he could tell she was blushing again.

The woman was clearly trying to kill him and he couldn't help but wonder how flushed she'd get during sex. Would it just be her cheeks or would that extend… *Nope.* Couldn't go there now. Not if he wanted his dick to stay under control. "Were you going to ask how old I am?" he asked.

She let out an embarrassed laugh. "You don't have to answer."

"Nah. I don't care. I'm thirty-two." After the Marines he'd done a fast-track in college, pushing himself to graduate early. Then he'd been hired by the FBI, had thought it was his dream job. Yeah, he learned the hard way that it wasn't. Not even close.

"You look younger."

He didn't have a baby face exactly, but without his beard he definitely looked to be in his mid-twenties. He used that to his advantage when necessary. "Yeah...so, you hungry?"

Smiling softly, she nodded.

And he knew that he was definitely screwed where she was concerned. He barely knew her but felt consumed with the need to protect her. He spent his time killing guys who deserved it, and she was this innocent, defenseless woman who tugged at all of his protective instincts. It was unnerving, but he wasn't going to walk away. He couldn't.

* * *

As she sat at the center island drinking a glass of wine, Hadley wondered if it had been a mistake to accept Axel's invitation to his place when she didn't know him, but when he hadn't balked at her giving his address to a friend, most of her tension had dissipated. She'd gotten pretty good at seeing through bullshit and charmers—charmers seemed to be the worst. Hiding their garbage under a pretty face and attitude. And while Axel seemed to have an edge to him, she wasn't scared of him.

The distinction was clear in her gut in a way she couldn't articulate. And she'd been trusting her instinct for a long time. Ever since one of her mother's boyfriends had tried to get too friendly with her.

Even being here with him now muted what had happened to her last night. Not so much that she could completely forget it, but she felt more balanced.

"So tell me more about your family," Axel said, glancing over from the stove.

Hadley wasn't sure how to respond. Earlier she'd almost called Brooks her half-brother, which was her tendency. But Brooks had made it clear that he thought of her as his sister, that there was no half about it in his mind. Something that absolutely warmed her heart. "That might be too heavy for first date stuff."

Taking another sip, she watched him cook at the stove. He had on gray pants and a dark sweater that did absolutely nothing to hide all the muscles underneath. Axel might be in finance but clearly he had a gym membership. And he could cook? The guy seemed too perfect. The simple veggie and skillet meal he was preparing smelled delicious.

"If you want to get technical we could consider it a second date." He grinned at her, a slow curving up of his delicious lips, and she felt it all the way to her core.

"I don't think me spilling coffee on you is considered a date." Not that she would know, since she hadn't been on one in forever.

"I'm going to count it," he said.

She laughed lightly. "Well I grew up with my mom on the West Coast. Only recently I met my father and brother. I knew they existed for a while..." She decided to hold some stuff back because this really did feel too deep for a getting-to-know-you-type of conversation. "I was really nervous to meet them both but they've been nothing but welcoming." That being an understatement. Her dad wanted to buy her a house and car, and just…no. It was too much and she wasn't comfortable with it. Not yet and maybe never. Though she knew it bothered her dad, and even Brooks was gently pressuring her to at least take a car. *Gah.* It was weird to have people who wanted to help her so generously when no one else ever had. And there didn't seem to be any strings attached either. Still, it was too much.

"That's incredible to meet your family after so long."

"Yeah, I know. I really wish they'd been in my life sooner." Because her relationship with her mother had been complicated and pretty toxic. And it wasn't as if she'd been able to escape that toxicity, at least not until she'd been old enough to move out. Even then she'd still been too afraid to reach out to her dad. Because she hadn't wanted to hurt her mom even though her mom hadn't cared about hurting her. But she wasn't going to think about that now and ruin this date.

"Where's your mom now?"

"She died a few years ago." And that was all she was going to say about that.

"I'm sorry. I…never knew my dad at all."

"What about your mom?"

He lifted a shoulder. "We weren't close." His body language changed ever so slightly, his posture became a bit more rigid, and she figured there was more to it than he wanted to tell her. Which was fine with her. There were some things she didn't like to talk about either and her familial relationships was one. "Let's talk about something different, then," she said, keeping her tone light.

"Okay, how is it that you're single?" he asked, pinning her with those incredible eyes as he leaned against the counter. Even when he picked up his water, he was focused on her.

She felt her cheeks flush hot. She cursed herself for her blatant reaction to him. It was insane. She'd never reacted to anyone like this before but around him her entire body simply went haywire. "I'll answer, but you get the same question from me. Honestly, I was so busy in college and then moving here, I haven't had time." Though if she'd wanted to *make* time, she would have. No one had interested her enough.

"I can understand that."

"Turnabout is fair play. I'm assuming you're single?" Something she probably should have asked him before agreeing to come here. He was in town on business after all.

He snorted and nodded. "Yes. Very single. I travel a lot and it makes relationships difficult."

Knowing that he wasn't permanently here and that he was being so honest with her, or at least she thought he was, made her open to being a little freer with him.

She'd never had a one-night stand before, and while she wasn't sure that she even wanted one, she was definitely thinking about it. But only with him. It felt kind of wrong and she wasn't sure why. Because everything about him felt really right in a bone-deep sort of way. There was something so sexy and, okay, a little fierce about him that turned her on.

Plus he had a seriously nice ass. Her mouth practically watered as she watched him at the stove and she felt like a pervert but didn't actually care. Because the man was fine.

After what had happened to her last night, maybe she would throw caution to the wind and have some fun. A lot of it.

CHAPTER FIVE

—If everyone knew what I was thinking, I'd get
punched in the face a lot.—

Skye stood with her hands on her hips as she watched
Gage work his magic on his laptop. "So?"

"Don't rush me," he growled.

Skye hated being between jobs. It made her antsy and
ready to run another ten miles. Considering she'd already run fifteen this morning, she feared that might be
overkill. But the whole situation with Hadley really
bothered her. Not enough to contact Brooks...yet. Because he was with his fiancée out of town on some sort
of work thing for her. Some kind of wedding conven-
tion, Skye wasn't really sure. And though she loved
Darcy, she wasn't really interested in anything to do with
weddings.

"Come on." Colt took her hand in his and pulled her
out of the room into the hallway. At the moment, it was
just the three of them at Redemption Harbor Consulting
in their converted warehouse. Leighton was away on a
small one-man job, Savage and Olivia were on their honeymoon, and Nova was gone for the day.

Skye wanted to snarl at her husband but didn't because he'd done nothing wrong. She was just being edgy

and annoyed and he didn't deserve her acting like a crazy person.

He gave her a wicked grin that made her toes curl in her boots. "If you're feeling edgy I can think of a way we can burn off some energy."

"Dude, I can still hear you guys!" Gage called out from his office.

Colt tugged her down the hallway. They'd actually only gotten busy once here, in her office. It had been after a particularly rough job, and they'd had the place to themselves and she'd wanted to burn off energy. Okay, who was she kidding—she'd wanted to screw her husband's brains out. Some days it was hard to believe she was actually married, much less alive. And she was so grateful to have him in her life. "This thing with her is just really bothering me," Skye said even as Colt pulled her into the break room instead of her office as she'd expected.

He pointed to the table. "Sit. And I know. I think the real reason you're bothered is because it's Hadley that it happened to."

"True enough." There was no reason to deny it. Hadley was the half-sister that Brooks recently found out he had, and she was absolutely adorable. And Skye worried about the girl's survival skills. Once when she'd asked Hadley how many exits were in the restaurant they'd been having dinner in, Hadley had given her a blank stare. Yes, they seriously needed to work on her observation and survival skills. "She's like a little puppy." Folding her arms across her chest, she frowned.

"That's a bit of an exaggeration." Colt pulled leftover pizza from the fridge and put it in the microwave. Yeah, he really did know her—and food was the way to her heart. "She put herself through college and was brave enough to reach out to her sibling and father, having no idea how they'd react to the news of her existence. She's not like us, but she's not a puppy."

"Well she's not answering her phone either. I called her and texted her earlier to check in and she said she was going on a date. A date!" After she'd been attacked in what Skye didn't think was a simple mugging gone wrong. All the details were too strange and she did not like strange.

Her husband leaned against the counter and folded his massive arms over his chest. "And that's a problem why?"

"If she's dating, we need to check out any potential men."

"You sound worse than Brooks."

"I wonder if he knows about her date." Skye pulled her phone out of her pocket but Colt—sneaky man—snatched it from her hand with panther-like reflexes.

"No," he simply said.

"I wasn't going to call him."

"Yes, but you were going to text him and probably his father."

She shrugged, not denying it. They both needed to know what had happened and lock Hadley down. At least until they could figure out what was going on.

Colt glanced down at his own phone as the microwave dinged. "Gage has something."

After grabbing her plate, Colt shoved both his phone and hers into his pocket and they headed back down the hallway.

"Really? You couldn't grab me anything?" Gage asked as they stepped inside, his gaze landing on Skye's plate.

"Fine, have mine." Skye set it on the desk next to him but he just eyed it with disdain and turned back to the computer.

"Pineapple does not belong on pizza," he muttered, pulling up a couple different screens. "What I've found isn't great. The power outage was localized to a very small portion of the college for a very short amount of time—right when Hadley was being attacked."

Tension rippled down Skye's spine. *Nope. Not good at all.*

"And the security feeds were erased as well, though if we break into the offsite company we could get them—if they haven't been corrupted."

"So we've got nothing basically." Other than something that smelled like shit.

"I didn't say that..." Gage pulled up another screen that showed a car pulling out of an entrance on the other side of the college. Four-door, generic-looking sedan, tinted windows and… It shifted to another screen and the front image of the driver was clear enough.

Not great. Man wearing a ball cap with a full-on beard was driving. Hands were gloved, which wasn't that strange even with it being March. Winter was still clinging on because Mother Nature was in a bitchy mood this year. "And, I got this too," he continued. Another screen showed the back of the car but the license plate was impossible to read because of mud smeared all over it.

Skye cursed again. "Damn it."

"Come on, be patient." Gage shook his head without looking at her.

Even Colt nudged her with his hip as he fought a grin.

"Fine." But she knew what he was doing. Gage liked to show off his computer skills—which she really couldn't blame him, considering how impressive they were. But still, if he had information on one of the men who'd been there last night she wanted to know right now.

"Say it," Gage said without looking up.

"Say what?"

"How awesome I am. Then I'll show you what I found."

"How about I refrain from punching you in the throat? And then you show me what you found."

Laughing, he said, "Fair enough."

A new screen popped up with a grainy feed showing a…marina, she thought. "Where is this? What is this?"

"Since you're being impatient, I skipped over all the other feeds I followed and I'm cutting right to the end. This guy is the only man resembling the description that Hadley gave you for the man who tossed her attacker in that trunk. Using what CCTVs and other video feeds I could hack into, I managed to track this guy—the vehicle, actually—to a local marina. And this is what I found. Keep watching."

Skye watched as the man parked, got out, and bent over his trunk for a few minutes. From the angle of the video, it was impossible to see what he was doing inside. When he stood back up, he lifted a huge bag—looked like a military-issue sea duffel—and hoisted it up. Then he made his way to a dock and from there it looked as if he got into a boat. But the angle was too far off to tell. "Anything else?"

"Nope. Other than the fact that the guy hasn't returned to the vehicle."

"Think there was a body in that bag?" Skye asked, even though she'd already come to that conclusion.

"Offshore is certainly a good way to dispose of a body, especially if it's weighted down," Colt said.

"Want to go check out the car?" she asked.

He nodded. "I love our Friday date nights."

Snorting, she clapped Gage on the shoulder once. "Thanks, man. That's incredible work. You know you can go home, right? It's freaking late."

He just shrugged. "Yeah…I'll get out of here soon but I'll keep an eye on the feeds through my phone. Buzz me if you need backup."

"Will do," Colt said, and grabbed her hand as he headed to the door.

* * *

As she sat on the couch with Axel, Hadley felt nervous for a multitude of reasons. The dinner he'd cooked was great, but she'd only eaten about half of what she normally would have because of the butterflies in her stomach.

Everything about him was different than the boys she'd dated in college. Everything was different about him, period. Despite his youthful appearance, his eyes told a different story. He looked almost haunted, and apparently she was a sucker for that because he was drawing her in like a moth to a flame or any other bad analogy she could think of.

"So which one do you think?" he asked, nodding at the screen where he scrolled through the newer movies available to rent.

When he'd asked if she wanted to stay longer and watch a movie she'd readily agreed. Because spending time with him was no hardship. The thought of going back to her little home or even the ranch alone wasn't appealing.

"The action one," she said because the thought of watching anything with a ton of sex in it with him made her squirm.

When he slid his arm around her shoulders, she leaned into him. She inhaled that spicy scent and swore it went straight to her head, making her a little dizzy. She'd only had one glass of wine so she couldn't blame her reaction on that at all. Not that she would. She was in charge of her own body and right now the last thing she wanted to do was watch a movie.

But she'd never made the first move or put any sort of moves on a man. She wasn't a virgin, but she also wasn't swimming in experience. And he made her nervous on so many levels. She was pretty sure he was attracted to her, but he was hard to read.

Somehow, from the time the opening credits started to before the characters had uttered a word of dialogue, she found herself tugged into his lap as he slid his fingers through her hair, cupping the back of her head. *Oh, yes please.*

Normally she pulled it up so that it was out of her way but she was glad she'd left her hair down tonight because she loved the sensation of him running his fingers through it. Everything about him was larger than life. Sexy, dominating and toe-curling. That was Axel.

Leaning forward slowly, he gently brushed his lips over hers, the sensation sending little pings of pleasure out to all her nerve endings. His lips were softer than she'd imagined and she wanted more than gentle right now. Her entire body felt as if she was coming apart at the seams with the need for...something more than this.

She wanted to straddle him, but she wasn't that bold. If anything, she felt out of her depth with him. Instead, she squeezed her legs together, hopefully subtly, as he nipped at her bottom lip. The effort did nothing to ease the growing ache between her legs. Apparently he had all the time in the world because he was taking his time kissing her, savoring it.

She slid her hands up his chest to rest on his shoulders. She wanted to dig her fingers into him but resisted. He seemed so relaxed and she was trying to retain some semblance of control and not pounce on him like a starving animal.

His other hand made its way down to her hip, where he held on to her with more pressure than necessary. And every part of her being liked it. He was holding on to her as if he didn't want to let go.

Good, because the feeling was mutual. And she wasn't going anywhere. Not right now anyway. She thought he might shift lower and push her dress up, but he continued teasing her tongue with his, his kisses sensual and expert.

The ache between her legs grew as he increased the intensity of his kisses.

Giving in to her earlier thought, she shifted and did straddle him, feeling a little out of control even as she moved. When she did, he let out a tortured-sounding groan and grabbed onto her hips as he rolled his against her. She had on panties and leggings under her dress but nothing could hide his erection. She shifted over his hard length, moaning at the feel of his erection teasing her clit. He groaned again, his grip on her hips tightening.

His chest rose and fell harshly as he pulled back, his eyes crystal clear as he watched her. "Stopping is the last thing I want to do, but I think we need to," he rasped out, sounding as tortured as she felt.

He wanted to stop? A hint of embarrassment slid through her. She wanted to ask why, but again, she wasn't that bold. Not yet anyway. And they *were* moving really fast. Even if she thought she might want a one-night stand, she wasn't completely sure, so yes, stopping was probably a good idea. Even if she really, really wanted to see where this led to.

In response, she nipped his bottom lip once and slid off him.

She loved that he groaned again, adjusted himself as she sat next to him.

Just like that, their surroundings came back into place and she realized the movie was still playing. She hadn't even heard the sound as they'd been making out, as she'd been grinding her body against his. She'd been too focused on his teasing tongue and the way he made her feel.

Not so subtly, he grabbed a pillow and put it over his lap as she curled into him. She giggled lightly but didn't say anything else as they settled in to watch the movie.

She wasn't sure what it was about him, but everything about tonight felt kind of perfect, even if she was still unsatisfied. But maybe that was a good thing, because she wanted more of this. More of him. And deep down, she was pretty sure she wanted more than one night.

She'd expected him to take her somewhere fancy and then maybe a movie afterward. Technically they'd done dinner and now a movie, but she liked this intimate atmosphere a lot better than if they'd gone out. Their conversation over dinner had felt more real than small, fake chitchat. Normally she didn't even open up to people because of the way she'd grown up, but with Axel she felt freer to be herself. Which was strange in itself. And for once she wasn't going to overanalyze why.

She settled her head on his shoulder and tried to pay attention to the movie instead of focusing on the sensation of his muscular body against hers. It was damn hard when she had a feeling that if they did get naked, it would be incredible between them. Maybe after the movie he would want to continue what they'd started. She could hope.

CHAPTER SIX

—Sometimes the wrong choices bring us to the right
places.—

Axel glanced over at Hadley who was dozing on his
couch. She'd dropped off a couple hours ago close
to the end of the movie and he hadn't wanted to wake
her. Her falling asleep had actually worked in his favor
since he was hoping that she would just stay the night in
the guest room if she woke up. It was a perfect excuse
not to take her home. Obviously he would if she wanted
to, but keeping her here would keep him sane—and her
safe.

He might actually get a few hours of sleep since he
wouldn't be constantly monitoring the cameras outside
her place.

At that thought he looked back down at his laptop.
He'd been working quietly on the other couch since she'd
fallen asleep. After draping a blanket over her, he'd
dimmed all the lights and could now focus on her cameras, plus the ones he'd set up at his rental condo, and
monitor for any incoming info from Isaac.

He finished fast-forwarding through another one of
the camera feeds outside her house. Nothing out of the
ordinary, just as the last one had been fine. Then he

started on the next one. Again nothing strange. Just random animals, because he'd set the sensitivity level of the cameras too high. So it was picking up all movement, including raccoons.

Pressing pause, his gaze strayed to her again even though he told himself not to want her, not to watch her. She was definitely not the type of woman for him.

But now that he'd gotten a taste of her, he was pretty certain he was screwed. Because she was everything he'd never known he wanted. God, she was going to hate him when he told her what he did for a living. Who he was. He just couldn't see a way around not telling her.

When an incoming message softly pinged, he pulled a new screen up. It was from his contact.

Got some movement at the marina, two individuals are checking out the car you ditched there. Watching them from the local camera.

Axel stilled at that message. That could mean any number of things. It could just be someone looking to steal it. He had left the keys in the ignition, after all. He'd wiped it down and if someone stole it, even better for him. There'd be so much DNA inside it that it would never be linked back to him. He'd thought about burning it, but ditching it had been easier given the location. And less likely to draw attention to it for a while. He hadn't wanted to return and grab it, putting himself at more risk. Because of the short nature of this job, he hadn't realized there was a camera on site. He'd found out about it afterward and was glad there was only one. Instead of tampering with it or removing it, he'd asked Isaac to hack into it and monitor it—for a fee, of course. The man didn't work for free.

Fingers moving quickly across the keyboard, he typed back, *Teenagers looking to steal it?*

The response was almost immediate. *No. They move like pros. Checking every inch of the car. It even looks as if they're dusting it for fingerprints.*

Yeah, good luck with that. He'd worn gloves and had been sure to have everything wiped down even before he'd grabbed the asshole who'd tried to take Hadley.

But he didn't like that someone was checking out his vehicle. It could mean he'd been spotted leaving the college, which was a possibility even though he'd been careful and had worn a hat, gloves and kept his ears covered. The beard had helped too. But this might mean that one of the kidnappers looking for Hadley was working with someone.

From the information he had on the other two men who'd been hired, it didn't seem plausible. He typed back, *What do they look like?*

I can't get a good visual—faces are covered by hats, and what are probably wigs covering their ears—and I'm 99% sure someone else is currently hacked into the camera system as well.

Well that was interesting. And not the kind of interesting that he liked. At least he didn't have anything to worry about as far as the body. He'd disposed of it well. And he hadn't returned to the marina, instead docking the boat elsewhere.

Send me any information including video footage. It was doubtful he'd recognize anyone disguised but it didn't hurt to watch it.

It'll cost you.

Yeah, no shit. Instead of typing what he thought, he simply said *Bill me.*

Any amount of money was worth keeping Hadley safe. But now it appeared as if things had gotten more complicated. He needed to get her somewhere more secure and he needed to tell her what was going on. Hell, he needed to tell her brother too. But...one more day with her. That was all he wanted. Maybe keeping her safe would balance his karma scale. Nah. He doubted it. He'd still protect her though.

As if she knew he was thinking about her, Hadley's eyes opened and she gave him a soft smile. Confusion flickered across her features as she sat up and looked around. Her dark hair was a little mussed and her dark eyes were sleepy. Yawning, she pushed the blanket down. "Did I miss the end of the movie?" Her voice was slightly raspy and sexy as hell.

"Yeah, it ended a few hours ago."

Her eyes widened. "I'm so sorry, I didn't mean to—"

"It's no worries. Since it's late do you just want to stay in the guest room? It's nice." The whole place was, in fact. It was secure enough and had a state-of-the-art security system. He lifted a shoulder as if it didn't matter to him when he really wanted her to stay put.

"Are you sure?" She seemed to hesitate.

"Yeah, I'd rather you stay here than get on the road this late. But whatever you want to do." *Please stay.*

"Do you have something I can wear?"

"Yeah. Everything I own will be too big but fine for sleeping in. Do you have plans tomorrow? I'll make sure you get home as early as you need." But he'd have to tell her the truth before he did that. There was no way around it. Because she needed to know, to be able to watch out for herself. Just...a few more hours with her. She could rest easy at least one night without the knowledge that someone wanted to kidnap her. Use her as leverage.

"I'd just planned to head out to my family's ranch and go horseback riding. With school being on break I'm taking advantage of the downtime."

Good. That should give him some time to contact Brooks and hopefully hunt down another one of the men sent after her once Axel knew she was safe with her brother.

"Do you want to come with me?" she asked, surprising him.

Or...he could do that. "I'd love to," he found himself saying. He would stay with her at the ranch, just to keep her safe. And then he'd tell her the truth.

He was so full of it he couldn't buy his own bull-shit. Yeah, he'd be keeping her safe, but he was a self-ish bastard for not telling her the truth right now. If he thought there was a chance she'd be harmed here or at her family's ranch then he'd tell her but...

He rolled his shoulders once and closed his laptop. "Let me grab you something."

Digging around in his suitcase he pulled out a plain T-shirt that would come at least to her mid-thigh and a pair of sweats she would have to roll over at the waist to keep up. He preferred to sleep naked at home but when he was on a job he wore clothes in case he was woken up by a threat.

God, his life was lonely. And she was this bright spot he was soon going to lose. Because in the reality he lived in, no way did they end up together.

When he returned to the living room, he found her folding the blanket and setting it neatly on the back of the couch. "I really don't mind going home. I feel as if I'm imposing."

"Trust me, you're not imposing." He just wished she'd be sleeping in his bed. But if that was going to happen, she needed to know who he was first.

Although then everything would be a moot point because he was certain she'd want nothing to do with him.

Her smile was soft and sweet. "Okay, then. Is that for me?" She nodded at the bundle of clothes.

"Yeah." He handed it to her as he showed her to the short hallway. The place was spacious but not so big she could get lost. "This is the extra bedroom." It had clearly been professionally decorated in a coastal theme. The kind of place that people traveling on business or for vacation would love to stay at. Not that any of that stuff mattered to him. But he was glad she seemed to like it.

"I'll just be a couple minutes." She looked indecisive, as if she wanted to say something more but changed her mind at the last second because she ducked into the room and shut the door behind her.

For a moment, he leaned his forehead against the door and tried not to fantasize about her undressing inside, putting on his clothes. Tried and failed. Because he really liked the thought of her wearing his stuff, being covered in his scent. Which was beyond primitive but...he didn't care.

Sighing, he stepped back and leaned against the wall in the hallway. He'd just tell her goodnight then put some distance between them. Yep, that was the plan.

Because he needed distance if he wanted to stay sane. Especially after that kiss they'd shared. She'd been so sweet and teasing and all he'd wanted to do was roll the two of them to the floor and thrust inside her until they were both sated.

Less than a minute later she opened the door wearing his much too big shirt and... *No. Pants.* She looked surprised to see him waiting. Shit, maybe he shouldn't have?

Damn it, he was in new territory here. This wasn't a typical first date, he knew that much.

"Hey, I just wanted to see if you had face wash or something? If you don't, it's not a big deal."

Axel forced himself not to look any lower, not to get a peek of her legs and all that bare skin. That was made easier when she stepped forward before he could even answer, raw lust in her gaze.

Swallowing hard, he shuddered as she pressed up against him, her hands settling on his shoulders. Before he realized it he'd moved, backing her up against the closest wall without actually touching her. His palms were flat against the wall as he looked down at her, caging her in even as he tried to order his feet to back up, to give her space.

Just walk away. And get her face wash or whatever she'd wanted.

But when she slid her hands over his chest, his entire body froze. He still didn't touch her though. Just curled his fingers against the wall. He could only watch as she slowly slid a hand down his covered chest, lower, lower...oh fuck. What was she doing? He hadn't remotely expected *this*.

Her dark eyes went heavy-lidded as she rubbed a hand over his erection. His cock ached, and he was desperate to feel her touching him, stroking him skin to skin.

"Can I?" she whispered, her own breathing harsh and out of control as she teased her fingers over him.

He let out a strangled sound that was supposed to be a yes. Thankfully she understood because, grinning wickedly, she unfastened his pants, shoved them down and...fuuuuuuck.

Feeling like an inexperienced teenager, he felt his balls pull up tight as she fisted his cock with her smooth palm. Yep, this was heaven. And he was about to die. What a way to go.

She wrapped her fingers around him and began stroking, slowly at first. All he could do was stare at her, his heart nearly seizing in his chest as she stroked up and down, over and over.

He hadn't remotely expected this. Fantasized about it? Yeah.

Her own breathing was harsh as she looked up at him. He arched slightly off the wall as she continued torturing him. He wanted to touch her everywhere and went to move but she just grinned, showing off that adorable dimple.

"No touching me," she whispered, her grip tightening.

That was...insanely hot. "Gotta kiss you."

"Okay." She'd barely got the word out when he crushed his mouth over hers, his need to taste her overwhelming.

He might not be able to touch her everywhere he wanted but this he could do. Her taste was sweet as he dominated her mouth, hungry to consume all of her.

This sexy, surprising woman who'd taken him off guard tonight.

He hadn't expected this boldness from her and he really, really liked it.

He'd never been so turned on in his life as he was right now. With her in his shirt, covered in his scent...he wanted to cover her in his come. Which felt raw, primal and kinda fucked up but he didn't care. He needed to mark this woman even if she could never be his. Even as he had the thoughts he cursed himself.

And started coming. There was no controlling it, not when she was pumping him with a perfect rhythm with her perfect hand. God, everything about her was perfect. As if she'd been made just for him. Which was stupid but... Pulling back, he groaned out her name as he came even harder in long jets against her hand and his stomach. His climax seemed to go on forever and for once, he had no damn control.

Shuddering as he finally came down from his high, he looked into her dark eyes, completely captivated. Yep, she owned him already, no doubt about it.

And he desperately wanted to give to her what she'd just given to him, to tease every inch of her body with his mouth and hands. God, he wished he had six hands right now. When he grasped the edge of her long shirt, ready to lift it over her head, she surprised him and placed her smaller hands over his.

"I'm not ready for more tonight." She almost looked apologetic, which stunned him.

He wanted to get on his knees and worship her pussy but if she didn't want more right now, that was okay too. This wasn't over though, not by a long shot. "Okay."

"Okay?" She seemed surprised.

"I want to taste you coming against my tongue but yeah, okay." He sure wasn't going to pressure her even if he felt selfish for being the only one to receive pleasure tonight. It made him feel off-balance and even more desperate to taste her. "We'll wait until you're ready." He cleared his throat. "I'm going to clean up but...do you want to stay in my bed tonight?"

She nodded, her cheeks pink. And just like that he started to get hard again. Axel had a feeling that was going to be a perpetual problem around her.

* * *

Skye stepped back from the abandoned car, frustrated that she and Colt had found nothing. Nothing they could use anyway. And they'd come prepared to search the vehicle. They'd done a luminol test in the trunk and there was blood visible with a black light, and if she was a betting woman she'd guess it was from the guy who'd attacked Hadley.

So no sleep lost there.

But they hadn't found any damn fingerprints. Which was flat-out wrong. So what the heck was going on? She couldn't wrap her mind around it. Someone attacked Hadley and then someone else incapacitated the attacker. But then what, he'd killed the attacker? Disposed of the body? Why? Who was this other man? Why had he helped Hadley?

"Let's see if we can get some of the blood and do a test on it," Colt said quietly as he glanced around.

The marina was out of the way, not one of the major ones in Redemption Harbor. It was quiet, which was no surprise since it was two in the morning. As far as she knew no one lived in any of the boats here. If they did, no one was moving around.

She and her husband were in disguise regardless. Nodding, she let her husband do his thing, cutting a couple swatches of the rug from the back of the trunk.

Once they were back in one of their company's vehicles—with an untraceable license plate—Colt said, "What's really going on with you?"

She wasn't certain what he meant as he steered out of the gravelly parking lot. "How so?"

"You're more amped up than usual about this. Is it because we don't have a job?"

They weren't in a lull exactly as far as work was concerned but everyone was busy with something at the moment and they didn't have anything pressing they needed to deal with. Which, as a former spy, she completely understood. There wasn't always going to be action, action, action. She definitely knew that more than most. In her downtime, she simply exercised a whole lot and cleaned her weapons. A lot of that had to do with her ADHD. She needed to keep busy and stay focused on something. It was also what made her so damn good at her job.

"I'm just worried about Hadley, that's all," she finally said.

Colt snorted softly. "Lie to yourself, don't lie to me."

She let out a sigh. The man always saw through her and had right from the start. "Fine. I don't know how to say it exactly. Before you, before us, and all of this, I never had people to worry about. Not really. And doing the job was easy."

Because helping strangers was easy, at least for her. And part of it was selfish. Doing the right thing made her feel good and she liked protecting people. That deep-seated need was embedded in her DNA, she guessed. She had this drive to simply make things better. If it was part of her DNA, she'd come by it naturally, considering her parents had been spies too.

But now... "I've got people I love and care about. A lot of people. It's weird. Because Hadley, Valencia, Mary Grace, her new baby, they're so damn innocent and I hate to use the word fragile because that's wrong, but I want to protect them all the time. And the world is messed up. Anything could happen to them any time of day. And I hate that I can't stop it."

Colt reached out and took her hand in his as he pulled up to a stop sign. "I know. I worry about them too."

"It's hard to compartmentalize and turn off my brain on the best of days."

He nodded. "It's one of the downsides to having so many people in your life. It's worth it though." He didn't phrase it as a question but she got the feeling that he was asking. As if he doubted she was glad about this huge change in their lives in the last couple years.

"Yes, it is definitely worth it. It's just made me very aware of my mortality and, okay, afraid for my friends." And she wasn't used to feeling afraid. She had only ever felt truly afraid when it came to Colt being in danger. Now she had *all* these people to worry about. It was a new, exhausting experience. She wasn't sure how anyone had kids, ever. She'd die of exhaustion worrying about them and fighting not to let it show.

He squeezed her hand again and lifted it to his mouth. Then he pressed a soft kiss to her knuckles. "I love you," he said.

"Right back at you." Pushing out a breath, she found herself calming. They'd figure out this mystery soon enough.

CHAPTER SEVEN

—Remember when I asked for your opinion?
Yeah, me neither.—

Hadley laid her head on Axel's chest, listening to the sound of his heartbeat. Strong and steady. Seemingly like the man.

After they'd gone horseback riding, they'd basically been vegging out by her brother's huge pool. It was kind of weird to be here without Brooks, but he'd made it abundantly clear that she should feel free to use this giant place as her own. He'd told her that he would be offended if she ever acted like a guest here, which yeah, just made her love him more. She wasn't sure how she'd gotten so lucky having him for a brother. Right now, however, she was a little glad he wasn't home. Because he'd probably go all overprotective crazy about Axel being with her.

It was strange not to have anything to do for a week. Heck, she'd been working since she was sixteen and normally worked over every single school break to save money. She hadn't been sure what she was going to do with herself, and now having all this free time with Axel was kind of incredible. She was really afraid she was falling for him, which was insane. They'd barely spent a day together. But he brought out this wild, fun side of her and she felt as if he really saw her.

Obviously there was so much they didn't know about each other but she wanted the chance to get to know everything about him.

"What's going on in that pretty head of yours?" Axel's fingers were lazy against her back as he rubbed up and down in a rhythmic fashion.

Cuddled up against him, there was nowhere else she wanted to be. "Nothing really, just enjoying today. It's kind of strange to be so lazy and do nothing."

The sky overhead was blue with just a few clouds scattered around but there was more warmth in the air today. Not enough to shed their jackets yet, but spring was truly coming and she was ready for it. It had been a bitterly cold winter.

"Are you expecting anyone?" he asked suddenly, his body stiffening ever so slightly.

"Ah...no. My brother shouldn't be back for a couple days. Why?" And her dad wouldn't be back until the next week since he was dealing with some business stuff in Florida. Even though he swore he was retired, Hadley didn't feel like he really was because he still worked a lot. Something she understood. She couldn't imagine not being busy.

"I thought I heard something." He sat up swiftly, his eyes scanning the patio and pool area. The Olympic-size pool glistened under the sunlight. Beautiful but still far too cold to get into. Even if it did have a heating system, Hadley wasn't sure how to work it and she wasn't getting in the thing anyway. "What's wrong?"

"Nothing." But the tense line of his jaw said otherwise as he pushed to his feet. Reaching out, he took her hand. "Let's head inside."

Okaaaaay. She wondered what was going on with him but didn't push as they headed for the back door. As they reached it, it swung open, surprising her. Even more surprising, Skye stepped out.

Hadley's eyes widened in surprise, but she was happy to see the other woman. "Hey! What are you doing here?"

Instead of answering, Skye swept a critical gaze over Axel. There was absolutely nothing sexual about her look either. Nope, she seemed as if she was sizing him up to literally fight him. Which wouldn't surprise Hadley, considering what she'd learned about Skye.

"Okay, since you're not going to answer me, Skye, this is my friend Axel. Axel, Skye."

Skye's eyes narrowed on him.

"Have you lost the ability to speak?" Hadley demanded.

Skye gave a tight smile. "Is this the guy you went out on a date with?"

Holy balls, what was wrong with Skye? "Uh, yes. Can we take this into the kitchen? Seems a little weird that we're all standing around here in the doorway with you looking a little like you want to punch my date." Hadley looked at Axel and rolled her eyes. "This is one of my older brother's friends. And she's my friend too. Though maybe after today I'm going to rethink that," she said, giving Skye a hard look.

Axel extended his hand to Skye. "Nice to meet you," he murmured.

Skye ignored his hand and stepped back to let them in.

Rolling her eyes again, Hadley wiggled past the other woman, dragging Axel with her. Maybe hanging out at the ranch hadn't been such a good idea. And she wasn't going to deal with getting grilled by her friend. Especially since Hadley was a grown-ass woman. She made her own decisions, and while she might love how overprotective her brother was, she wasn't going to put up with any garbage about her personal life. Not from anyone. Because she was under the impression that her brother and his friends thought she was helpless. In reality, she'd been taking care of herself for far longer than she should have been, thanks to a mom who hadn't given a crap whether she'd eaten or not.

As they stepped inside, Colt came in from one of the other entries. He smiled when he saw them, nodded politely at Axel. "Hey, I'm Colt, Skye's husband. What are you up to Hadley, enjoying your spring break?"

"Hey," she said, stepping over to give him a hug. She swore he was usually the only sane one of the bunch. "Colt, this is Axel and yes, I'm enjoying my spring break. What are you guys up to?" she asked as the two men shook hands.

They seemed to be sizing each other up, but it was much more subtle than what Skye Crazypants had been doing.

"Just stopping by Brooks's office to grab something. Saw an unfamiliar truck in the driveway and wondered how anyone got past his security."

Axel cleared his throat. "I've actually got to head out but it was nice to meet you guys. Hadley, want to walk me out?"

Disappointment rushed through her, but she tamped it down. He'd gotten a few texts earlier but had ignored them. She knew he was in town for interviews so either he had to get to one or was freaked out by Skye's weird behavior and was leaving. She couldn't actually blame him.

Once they were outside, she said, "I'm really sorry about my friend. She's being a total weirdo."

He snorted. "It's no big deal. It's clear she cares about you."

"Yeah..." Hadley started to say that Skye was normally, well, normal, but that was a lie. She'd heard Mary Grace say that she was crazier than a bag of cats. Often.

"Listen...I've got to prep for an interview. Can I ask you something that will make me sound like a weirdo too?"

She laughed lightly as she nodded. "All right."

He took a deep breath. "Can you promise to stay here? At your family's ranch? Until I can pick you up?"

"Ah...yeah, I hadn't planned on leaving. Why?" They'd driven here separately so she had her car—not that it really mattered since Brooks had multiple vehicles here that he'd said were always at her disposal.

"I can't tell you. Yet. But I do need to talk to you as soon as I wrap up this next interview." His phone buzzed again in his pocket.

She frowned. "What's going on? Are you in any kind of romantic relationship?" She'd already asked him but she wanted to ask again, to gauge his reaction.

He blinked once, clearly surprised. "What? No. Shit, no. I..." His phone buzzed again. "I've just got some stuff to deal with, but promise you won't leave."

She really wanted to push him but there was a sort of desperation in his clear eyes and apparently she was a sucker for him. "Okay, I promise."

Relief bled into his gaze before he bent his head, brushing his lips over hers. She felt the kiss all the way to her core as butterflies exploded inside her. Man, a simple kiss and her knees were weak. This man had completely gotten under her skin.

"I've got my phone on me. Call me for anything," he murmured as he stepped back. "If I don't answer right away I'll call back."

"Okay." She stayed outside as he left, watching him head down the long driveway. To get onto the ranch she'd had to put in the code her brother had given her at the main gate—a couple miles away—and an alert had been sent to Brooks's phone that someone new was on the property. He'd know it was her because of the code and because she'd texted him, letting him know she was here. At least Axel wouldn't have to enter a code to leave. The sensor would let him out.

A cool breeze rolled over her as she headed back inside, making her wrap her arms around herself. It was silly but she already missed Axel. Don't be stupid, she ordered herself. And getting too attached to him would be just that. Stupid. They were just having fun and he would be leaving soon. Something she needed to remember. She was so curious why he wanted her to stay put and wondered if it had something to do with his current job. Maybe he wasn't in finance but something else, like law enforcement, and he wanted to tell her? Gah, she was just pulling stuff out of the air now.

"So what the heck was that craziness?" Hadley asked Skye as she stepped back into the kitchen to find the other woman making a sandwich with far too many layers of meat and cheese.

"What are you talking about?"

"You were so rude to him. And you looked a little bit like you wanted to punch him in the face."

The other woman shrugged, completely unapologetic. "I was simply sizing him up. I promised Brooks that I would look out for you. So that's what I did. If the guy can't handle it, he's not worth it."

"I don't think that's what Brooks meant by watching out for me."

Skye shrugged again, making Hadley even crazier.

She took a deep breath. "So does that mean you're going to cease acting like a normal human being anytime I bring a friend by?"

"That man is not a friend. Maybe your lover, but not a friend."

Hadley felt her cheeks heat up and shot a quick glance at Colt, who was definitely ignoring her as he opened the refrigerator, probably to avoid her gaze.

"What I do with my personal life is my business. Not Brooks's, not yours, not anyone's. And you better not have Gage run his information or hack his life or...whatever it is you guys do." She knew her brother and the rest of the people who worked for Redemption Harbor Consulting engaged in some gray-area behaviors, and she wasn't quite sure what their consulting consisted of other than "security issues" but she was pretty sure they broke the law. Probably more than she wanted to think about.

Skye snorted and took a big bite of her sandwich.

To quote Mary Grace, oh, sweet baby pandas. Because Mary Grace had been right. Skye was going to drive her insane at times. Hadley figured that was something she'd have to learn to deal with. She took another steadying breath. "I'm dead serious. You're not going to do anything about him. I'll sleep with whoever I want to."

Skye set her sandwich down as she swallowed. "So you're sleeping with him?"

Damn it. "No. But even if I was, it wouldn't matter. I haven't dated in forever and haven't had fun in a long time so don't mess with me. Whatever I do with him is *my* business." She knew she definitely didn't scare Skye whatsoever so she was surprised when the woman nodded.

"I will respect your privacy as much as I can."

Definitely not the answer Hadley had wanted, but it would have to do. Later she was going to have a serious talk with Brooks and ask him to never, *ever* task Skye with watching out for her in the future. "So what are you guys really doing out here?"

"We told you," Colt said. "By the way, have you eaten yet? Since Skye made only herself a sandwich I can whip something up for the two of us."

Skye's eyes widened. "You said you weren't hungry!"

Colt just gave his wife a look that Hadley couldn't decipher before turning back to her.

Laughing lightly, Hadley shook her head. "I'm fine, but thank you."

"Are you going to stick around here for a while?" Skye asked.

Since she wasn't going to tell them about the strange conversation she'd had with Axel, she simply nodded. "Yeah, with school out, I plan on doing absolutely nothing for a week." She also planned to hang out with Axel as much as possible but she wasn't going to bring him up again.

"Great. Are you okay with us being out here tonight?" Skye asked, her expression suspiciously neutral.

Which made Hadley think she was up to something. "Of course." But if Axel called and wanted to do something, she was so gone. She really wanted to finish what they'd started at his place. Today at the ranch he'd been surprisingly hands-off. He'd been affectionate but he hadn't pushed for anything more. While she appreciated that, she wanted more.

And she couldn't help but wonder if he did. She just hoped that whatever it was he wanted to talk to her about, the reason he'd wanted her to sit tight, was a good thing.

CHAPTER EIGHT

—Live, laugh, love. If that doesn't work, load, aim, fire.—

Axel hated leaving Hadley, but he knew one thing for sure: she would be safe on the ranch. He didn't recognize the woman, Skye, but he knew who the man was even if Colt Stuart hadn't recognized him. They'd worked parallel on an operation years ago when Axel had been with the FBI, and Colt with the CIA. And they'd only ever crossed paths once during that op—in a conference room where they hadn't spoken to each other at all. Axel had been sporting a beard then too. Still, there was a chance Colt would remember him eventually. He'd heard through the grapevine that Colt had left the Agency a while ago.

Right about now he wondered what the hell Colt and his wife had been doing at the ranch and how they had ties to Brooks. Clearly they were friends with Hadley so he felt better knowing Colt would be there.

Damn it, he should have dug deeper into what Brooks was into now. He'd been too focused on Hadley and any potential threats. As soon as he could, he'd do his own damn research on the man instead of having his tech guy do a run.

Getting off the ranch was easy enough, though it took everything inside him to leave Hadley. At least she'd promised to stay put. Which gave him time to take care of what he needed to—hunting down one of the men who'd been sent after her. Then he would tell her the truth. He had to. Otherwise he was keeping her in danger and he simply couldn't do that. Especially since the third man hired to kidnap her should be getting into the country tomorrow—according to his contact.

She would definitely kick him out of her life after, but that was something he was willing to deal with. Because keeping her safe and alive was more important than anything else.

He was still stunned at what she'd done last night, how she'd taken over and stroked him to orgasm. And he was fairly certain she'd stunned herself. It had been hot as fuck and he wanted more of it. More of her. He wanted to taste all of her.

When his phone buzzed again, he quickly scanned through the last round of texts to see if he'd missed anything and slid his earpiece in.

Isaac answered on the first ring. "About time."

Axel wasn't going to apologize because he paid the man. "What've you got?" Because Isaac's last text said he had something good.

"Martin Johnson. Your second hitter. Found him through a facial recognition scan. Got a hit from the DMV. Eighty-three percent accuracy."

Yeah, that worked for Axel. He knew Johnson's reputation. He wasn't the best, but he also didn't suck at his job either.

"I tracked him using the license plate of the car he rented. It's not under his real name. But I did a search on the name he used to rent the car and found the same person rented a house on the outskirts of Redemption Harbor. He was headed in that direction last time I caught him on a camera, but he might not have ended up there. Or even if he did, he could have left since then. I'm not sure where he is but now you have his address and I'll send you the alias he's using and everything else I found."

"Good work."

"Why are you going to all this trouble to hunt these guys down?"

Axel was surprised by the man's curiosity and he certainly wasn't going to tell Isaac the truth. They worked together, but they weren't friends. "It has to do with another job. Someone wants to keep their target safe. And they pay better."

"Figured as much. I'll let you know whatever else I find."

"Thanks." It didn't take him long to reach the rental house. It was on the outskirts of town, just like Isaac said. A quiet area with houses located along a riverbank. Each house he passed looked older, probably built in the seventies, but they were all kept up with neat lawns and a menagerie of garden gnomes. And each place had an actual yard with a lot of space.

Scanning the neighbors' houses on either side of his target's house, he gauged that at least one person was home, given the Ford F150 out front as he pulled into the driveway of Johnson's rental. Shouldn't be a problem, but he'd need to ditch this vehicle once he was done here, just to be safe.

Ball cap and sunglasses on, he stepped outside and leaned against the driver's side door as he dialed a number he had on file for Johnson. The guy had rented the place for a month, giving himself plenty of padding if the job took longer than normal. According to the info Isaac had sent him, the house was owned by a couple who'd retired in Florida. Now they rented it out using a home rental site. And Johnson had declined the house cleaning service according to the contract, so at least Axel wouldn't have to worry about some cleaning crew showing up unexpectedly.

Johnson answered on the second ring. "Yeah?"

"It's O'Sullivan." Johnson knew Axel's real name, just as he knew Johnson's. That wasn't always the case in this industry, but there were a handful of men and women whose real identities he was aware of.

A pause. "What the fuck do you want?"

"I'm in the driveway of your rental digs. Don't shoot me if I knock on the front door."

Another pause, then Axel watched as the blinds on the left window slightly moved. "What are you doing here?"

"Need to talk to you about your current job."

"So talk."

Axel glanced around, then lifted a hand as if waving at a neighbor. The person would be out of the line of sight for Johnson but he'd still think someone was out here.

"Damn it. Hold on. You want to come in, lose your weapons."

"Already did." Without pause he ended the call and strode toward the front door. As he moved he subtly unzipped his jacket and opened it up. When he stepped onto the front porch, he took it off and moved in a slow circle. If anyone was watching they'd probably wonder what he was doing but he wasn't worried about it.

Less than ten seconds later, the door opened with Johnson standing back in the shadows, a SIG in his hand. "Step inside slowly."

Axel rolled his eyes, because the guy was overreacting, but did as he said. "I'm going to set my jacket on this table and I'll lift my arms." He wasn't going to attack the guy. Not unless Johnson pushed his hand.

Nope. He was going to appeal to Johnson's greed. Because it usually worked with guys like this. Not that he had any room to get up on a high fucking moral horse since he killed people for money too. But he had a code at least and he only knew half a dozen others who did as well. It was why Hadley's contract had ended up in his hands in the first place. Someone had known it looked wrong and hoped he'd take care of it. AKA help her.

Getting that file had changed his life in a way he'd never imagined. He was going to make sure it saved hers.

He waited patiently as Johnson holstered his weapon and scanned him with a wand for any electronic devices. Johnson took out Axel's phone, removed the battery and set the pieces on the table next to his jacket. Then he scanned Axel's jacket. When he was satisfied, he set the wand down and faced off with him.

"How did you find me?"

Axel scoffed. He wasn't going to give away any secrets, something Johnson would know. "I'm here to make you an offer. Walk away from your current contract and my employer will double your fee."

In his mid-thirties, Johnson was about five feet ten, well built and a decent-looking guy. Unlike some of the men in their profession, he didn't look rough. Nope, he clearly took care of himself or at least didn't abuse his body with drugs or alcohol. Johnson ran a hand over his closely cropped dark hair. "That's an interesting offer."

Axel shrugged. "Take it or leave it. It's a one-time offer."

"Who hired you?"

He scoffed again. "Come on." They both knew Axel wasn't going to answer.

Johnson tapped his chin once. "I saw you out with her. I wondered why you were in town. Thought you must have started slumming it and taken this job."

Yeah, because Johnson at least knew that Axel wasn't going to kidnap a woman. That wasn't his MO. "Nope. Got a client who wants to keep her alive. So walk away and you still get paid. Win-win for everyone."

"What happens when word gets around that I don't finish my jobs? Work will dry up."

Axel snorted now. "Please." They both knew that wasn't true. Johnson was just looking to get paid more. Something Axel had planned on. Greedy bastard.

He leaned against the nearby doorframe "You doing her? She's hot."

Axel simply kept his expression neutral, even though he wanted to smash his fist into Johnson's face for that comment.

Johnson sighed and tilted his head once, telling Axel to follow him. "Let's talk in the kitchen. I need a beer."

Axel's instinct kicked in as he followed after the man. Something was up, but he wasn't sure what yet. Johnson was known for being semi-choosy about his jobs and not being a total psycho. It was why Axel had approached him like this.

He tensed as Johnson opened the refrigerator door, ready for the man to pull out another weapon. Instead he pulled out two domestics and handed one to Axel. Though he had no intention of actually drinking it, he took what was offered. He could pretend to be civil.

"I'm not walking away for double but I will for quadruple. I know what the bitch's father is worth and I'm guessing he's the one who hired you."

Axel simply lifted a shoulder, which would look like a confirmation.

"Figured as much. So...quadruple it and I'm gone. I like easy money."

Paying off Johnson was going to deplete a hell of a lot of his savings, but it was worth it. Hadley was worth it. After Johnson was out of the picture, that would be two down and one more left to get rid of. By whatever means necessary. He just wanted this done with no mess. "Fine. My client will need to know where to wire the funds. And I'm going to watch you call in and cancel with your own client."

"So how is she?" Johnson asked as he ripped a piece of paper from a Post-it pad on the fridge.

Axel stayed quiet.

"Come on. I'd been looking forward to fucking her before handing her over to that moron."

Axel forced himself not to react. "Seriously? You'd damage the merchandise?" He hated talking about Hadley like that but he needed to play a role. Even if he wanted nothing more than to wipe that smug look off Johnson's face. With his fists. Repeatedly.

"I could have done it without damaging her...much." He snorted as he finished writing the account number down. "Not like it matters. I get the feeling my client plans on hurting her if he gets his hands on her."

Axel tried not to react but his emotions must have shown on his face, and whatever Johnson saw, he didn't like because he stiffened. So much for feigning civility. Dropping the paper, Johnson stepped forward, clearly ready to attack.

Using all his training, Axel tossed the full beer at Johnson, knowing exactly what the man would do. It was human instinct unless you had the training—and Johnson didn't. Johnson's hand snapped out to catch the beer and Axel attacked like a rabid animal.

He couldn't dredge up any remorse for what he was doing either. He'd wanted to do this the easy way, but screw this monster. This man had wanted to rape and hurt Hadley before turning her over to another monster. And he'd said it so easily, as if he'd done it before. Probably had.

Which just sent Axel into full-on attack mode. As Johnson lost focus, reaching for the damn bottle like an amateur, Axel struck out, slamming his boot into the man's knee.

Screaming, Johnson fell back as his leg buckled, slamming against the Formica countertop. He wasn't down though. With wicked speed he withdrew the SIG he'd holstered. Before he could fully raise it, Axel slammed a fist against his face.

Johnson blocked with his other arm, but it threw him off-balance. He fell back again and Axel broke the wrist holding the weapon, making him scream again.

Needing the guy to shut the hell up, he pounced on him, slamming his head against a cabinet. Wood cracked and splintered even as blood spurted everywhere. Wrapping his arm around Johnson's neck from behind, he utilized a move he'd done more times than he cared to think about.

Breaking a neck wasn't as easy as it looked in the movies, not when someone was struggling, but Johnson was screaming, so caught up in his own pain he was simply thrashing around like a fish.

Pathetic.

No wonder he'd washed out of the army. Axel broke his neck, relief coursing through him at the familiar sound of it snapping.

Instantly Johnson's body went limp, turning into a dead weight.

Axel let him drop to the tile floor, inwardly cursing the mess. He had to dispose of the body and clean everything up now. Including repairing the damage he'd done. Then he'd have to clean out everything Johnson had at the house. He couldn't leave his own truck in the driveway too long either. No, he'd have to move it somewhere, then return here. He assumed that Johnson had his rental in the garage so he'd use that to dispose of the body. He'd just leave it in the trunk and set it on fire somewhere remote. Johnson would be found eventually but Axel didn't care about that as long as it couldn't be traced back to him.

All this was going to take time. Time he'd have to be away from Hadley. Which was why he'd wanted to do this the easy way. Dammit.

Hurrying back to the foyer, he put his battery back in his phone and texted her.

Still prepping for the interview. How's the rest of your day going?

She answered almost immediately. *Good, reading by the pool. Wish you were with me.*

God, he loved how honest she was. No games for her. *Wish I was too. I'll see you soon though. Text you as soon as I'm free?*

Please do. I'd like to do dinner tonight if you can?

I'm in. I'll call you when I'm on the way. He didn't plan to take her anywhere because he didn't want her out in public. But he would be telling her the truth. Most of it anyway. That someone wanted her kidnapped and she needed to stay at her family's ranch where she'd be safe.

Of course then she'd tell him to fuck off, though probably in nicer words than that. And that would be that. He'd lose her.

He told himself that it shouldn't matter. That they barely knew each other. But it *did* matter. The thought of losing her now, when this little spark between them had just started… Hell. He felt like he was losing everything.

CHAPTER NINE

—Honesty is better than sugar-coated bullshit.—

Axel reread the text he'd just seen from Hadley. Even though he knew it wasn't going to change. When he saw the timestamp from a couple hours ago, his stomach tightened. She'd received a call from a vet she knew through her school program who'd asked her if she wanted to shadow a surgery. And she'd said yes. Because of course she would. She had no idea there was a threat against her.

He'd texted her back and hadn't heard from her in ten minutes. It wasn't like she owed him any response at all. Regret filled him, eating away at his insides like acid as he cursed his own selfishness. He should have told her. From the tracker he saw on her vehicle, she was close to her home so he was headed in that direction. She had to be okay.

His phone buzzed and when he saw her name, the relief that flooded his system was like a tsunami.

Headed home, surgery went well. Dog made it.

He texted back immediately. *Good. I can meet you at your place if you'd like?* He'd already been monitoring the cameras and hadn't seen any movement. That was something at least.

Sounds good. I'm going to pick up Chinese food. Do you want some?

He didn't want her stopping anywhere. *I'll grab it, just head home.*

If you're sure, I'll take you up on that. I like orange chicken :-)

Got it. He paused, then added a smiley face emoji which was...out of character.

Fuck. He was telling her as soon as he brought the food over. He'd stop by, give her the food, and just get it all out. Then insist that she head to her brother's ranch—and he'd follow her to make sure she got there okay. He was sure she wouldn't balk at leaving her place once he told her someone wanted to kidnap her. But he still dreaded having to actually tell her, especially to her face.

It didn't take long to get the food and get to her house. In fact, on his monitor he'd seen her arrive only two minutes before he pulled into the driveway.

Some of the tension inside him eased, until Brooks Alexander knocked on the passenger side door. *Well, hell.*

It took a certain kind of person to surprise him and Brooks definitely had the training. Axel unlocked the doors and remained still, keeping his hands visible as the other man slid into the leather passenger seat.

Brooks's expression was dark. "Axel O'Sullivan. What the hell are you doing with my sister?"

No way to ease into this. "Someone wants to kidnap her. I've taken out two of the men hired. One more is still after her but won't be arriving until tomorrow per my contact. I've been trying to figure out who hired them but no luck so far."

Brooks blinked once, letting his surprise show for only a second. "How did you come by this information?"

"Do you know what I do for a living now?" He certainly wasn't going to spell it out for the man but he needed to know what he was working with here.

"Yes."

Okay then. That was...interesting. Not many people knew. But Brooks was not only trained, he had a lot of money and resources. He cleared his throat. "My pseudo-handler sent me her contract because, well, he didn't like it. He thought I'd take care of it because..." Because it wasn't the first time he'd stopped something like this. Axel didn't say that though. "Anyway, when I looked at her familial relationships, I realized you guys had to be related because of your father." Even if they did have different last names.

Brooks's jaw tightened and he seemed to struggle for a long moment with what to say. "You still haven't answered what you're doing with her—what you were doing at my house. I know what you do but I also know you wouldn't hurt a woman. So why didn't you just come to me with all this instead of involving her?"

Axel turned to look out the driver's side window at Hadley's little house. It was adorable, like her. And it was probably the last time he'd see it in person. He turned back to Brooks. "I got to town as soon as I could and planned to warn her in person."

When he didn't say any more Brooks raised an eyebrow. "And?"

"And then I met her. I like her. A lot."

Brooks's jaw tightened again, and that clichéd statement that if looks could kill? Yeah, Axel would be dead. No doubt about it.

"She's sweet and kind," Axel added, as if he even needed to. Anyone who'd ever met her would know that. She was sunshine and rainbows, things he'd never had in his life. Things he knew he didn't deserve. But apparently he was holding on to the insane hope that just maybe he could have her.

"Yeah, no shit. She's not for you. Who does she think you are?"

"I didn't lie about my name but she thinks I work in finance, that I'm in town looking for a new job. How did you find out about me?"

For a long moment Brooks didn't answer and Axel figured he wasn't going to. Finally the other man spoke. "You met a couple of my friends at the ranch. They ran your fingerprints—and one of them remembered you from an op after that. It took some digging, but one of my people put the pieces together and figured out what you do."

The water bottle by the pool. He'd forgotten about it. And he'd wiped down everything else he'd touched. Damn it. That was the kind of stuff that got you killed. He was too distracted right now. Hadley did that to him. Running his fingerprints wasn't something civilians did so that left a bunch of unanswered questions. Too bad for him he was pretty certain that Brooks wouldn't answer shit right now. "Was that you at the marina?"

"Why'd you leave the FBI?" A blunt question from Brooks. Apparently he was going to ignore Axel's other question.

All right, then. He turned away, not willing to tell the other man anything. "It doesn't matter and the only person I'll tell is Hadley."

"You're not going to tell her anything. You're going to leave right now and get the hell out of town. And you can send me any information you have on who wants my baby sister kidnapped." There was a wealth of protectiveness in his words.

Axel approved of Brooks's attitude. Hadley should be protected. He didn't want to leave but the other man was right. He wouldn't actually be leaving town until he knew she was safe, but he would stay away from her. "I set up multiple cameras around the perimeter of her place. I can send you the login so you can monitor her. And I can send you the information on the two dead men. But I...I'm not leaving until I know she's safe. Unless you're planning on going to the cops, you can use me to track down who wants her kidnapped. Or to keep her safe. Whatever."

Brooks snorted at the very idea of getting law enforcement involved. "No cops. So...that was you at the school?"

"Yeah... Why doesn't your father have her in a better place? Somewhere with more security?" Because their family was loaded. And it pissed Axel off that she wasn't in some ivory tower with armed guards and a hell of a lot better security than she had.

"Are you kidding? She insists on paying for herself if we go out to lunch. She's so stubborn." His expression softened for just a second. Then Brooks's gaze traveled past him for a fraction of a moment and Axel turned to see Skye walking toward the front door.

There was no way the woman could see past the tinted windows of the truck, not when it was this late, but she still saluted him with her middle finger before rushing up the stairs. "What's she doing here?"

"When she sent me the information on the man who was hanging around Hadley, I got here as soon as I could. I was your distraction while Skye did recon to see if you'd brought anyone with you. And we'll take care of things from here. Now send me what you've got and get the hell out of town."

Axel didn't say anything as Brooks got out of his truck and slammed the door.

Leaning back against the seat, Axel watched the other man step inside Hadley's house. He should leave, he really should. But first, he grabbed the Chinese food and headed to her front door. Putting it on the front stoop, he turned to leave and the door swung open. Hadley stood there, her expression confused and hurt.

Seeing the hurt on her face…she might as well have slapped him.

"Was our first meeting planned? Or was it accidental?" she blurted. Behind her, Skye and Brooks stood there, clearly pissed.

He shoved his hands into his pockets. "The whole coffee-spilling thing was accidental, but meeting you, yeah, that was definitely planned." Of course he hadn't planned to fall for her.

Her eyes were full of accusation as she stared up at him. "Was anything we shared real?"

He blinked at her question. "Yes. *Everything* we shared was real. I didn't lie about my name or any of the other stuff I told you. Except…what I do for a living."

Behind her, Skye cleared her throat. "Just bring the food in and get inside." She gently took Hadley's upper arm and tugged her back as Axel stepped inside with the food. He handed it to Brooks, which just seemed to annoy the man even more.

Without taking his eyes off Axel, Brooks set the food down on the small foyer table. Axel had eyes only for Hadley.

"So why are you here, really?" she asked, her arms wrapped around herself. Wearing jeans and a button-down flannel shirt and her hair pulled up in a ponytail with no makeup, this was the college girl he'd seen from the original file on her. This was the innocent-looking woman he'd had to come meet in person because there was no way in hell she should have been targeted for anything.

"My name is Axel O'Sullivan. Like I said, I didn't lie about that. I used to work for the FBI. Now..." He drew in a breath, steeled himself for her reaction. Because it wasn't going to be pretty. "I kill people for a living."

CHAPTER TEN

—One day or day one.—

Hadley blinked at his harsh words, sucking in a sharp breath. Yep, her reaction was exactly as he'd predicted. Exactly as Axel deserved. He'd known that his time with her was limited, but it didn't lessen the sting any. Not when she was everything he'd ever wanted. Even if he hadn't known it until he'd met her.

"Seriously? You're skipping over all the details?" Skye asked. "Come on, everyone let's do this in the kitchen. The food smells good and I'm freaking starving. And you are going to tell her more. Because I read your file and it's interesting. So you don't get to tell her that you're some jackass assassin without giving her all the details."

Having no choice, Axel followed, and tried not to feel like he was going to his execution. He hadn't planned on telling Hadley anything else because it would've sounded like an excuse, as if he was trying to justify what he did for a living. And he didn't want to do that. Because he wouldn't try to justify it. He'd made choices and he lived with them. Even if he was alone.

Inside the kitchen, Hadley was the only one who sat at the small island countertop while Skye started pulling takeout boxes from the bags.

"The orange chicken is Hadley's," he said, looking at Skye.

Skye gave him a curious look but simply nodded as she started grabbing plates. Brooks didn't do anything other than hover near him, looking angry. Not that he was scared of the other man. No, the only person he was scared of was the gorgeous young woman sitting right in front of him.

"So you...*kill* people?" Hadley's voice shook slightly.

"He killed two men who wanted to kidnap you. Probably do worse than that to you. We had someone run the blood of one of the guys he killed and he was not a good man. He'd have definitely hurt you." Skye's words were so matter-of-fact that everyone turned to stare at her. She lifted a shoulder. "Not the most noble profession but he did protect you."

Axel blinked at her words. He wasn't even sure how the woman knew what he'd told Brooks earlier until he saw the small earpiece in Brooks's ear. Damn it, of course that was how they were communicating. Which no doubt meant there were more people outside. Probably putting a tracker or some bullshit on his truck. So he had to ditch the truck soon. And damn it, he should have just burned that car. It had to be how they'd gotten a blood sample of one of the dead hitters.

Skye picked up a potsticker. "Tell me I'm wrong," she said when he didn't respond.

He looked at Hadley, saw a trace of fear in her gaze and simply said, "Both men wanted to kidnap you."

"Are you the bearded guy from school?"

He nodded.

"Thank you for what you did." Her softly spoken words surprised him.

"You don't ever have to thank me for anything." Definitely not for what he'd done.

"So are you going to tell her why you quit the FBI?" Skye asked, pushing a plate of food in front of Hadley.

Hadley barely glanced at it before her gaze fixed back on Axel.

"Difference of opinion on how procedures should be handled." And that was all she needed to know.

Skye rolled her eyes, exasperated. "Fine, I'll tell her."

"Damn it, Skye, just leave it alone," Brooks snapped. "So he can just leave. It doesn't matter what his reasons were. He doesn't belong here and he's not welcome."

Skye looked at him, her head tilting slightly to the side. "Really? He *saved* Hadley. Of all people, you're gonna judge him? Because you and I have no room to judge anyone when it comes to—"

Brooks cut her off with a sharp shake of his head.

"So," Skye continued, turning away from Brooks to face Axel, "from what I gather, you discovered that one of the top men in a criminal organization your team was trying to bring down was a serial rapist and murderer."

"How—"

"From multiple contacts and your personnel file," she said, cutting him off. "Yes, I'm good enough to have your personnel file. And unless you're going to tell her, then I get to finish this. So, you wanted to stop this guy. But your higher-ups decided that they wanted the bigger fish. His big, bad boss." She snorted. "Sounds exactly like something those assholes with the FBI would do too. Stop me if I'm wrong."

He simply shrugged. She was doing fine all by herself. How the hell had she gotten his personnel file? And more importantly, how the fuck did they know what he did for a living? It wasn't common knowledge and Brooks would have had to do more than "put the pieces together" to figure it out.

"That's what I thought. So," she continued, watching Hadley, "your boy over here wanted to do the right thing. But his bosses considered those women expendable since they were prostitutes. I guess the Feds figured they didn't deserve the right to live because of their chosen profession. Axel disagreed and tried to go over his head. Didn't work because the grandboss wanted the head of the criminal organization more than a serial rapist and killer. The guy went on to kill six more women before they finally brought him down. And not all of those women were prostitutes, which is the only reason they brought him in. Not that it matters, because they should've listened to Axel right away. And the kicker is, they didn't even bring down the bigger fish." Disgust filled her voice. "Does that about cover it?"

"Yeah."

Hadley turned to look at him and said, "So what happened? How did you go from that to killing people?"

He looked at her for a long moment, unable to find his voice. "I didn't, not right away anyway. But I turned in my resignation after that. I took a job with them because I believed in a cause, but the people in charge really only cared about getting their faces in the news."

Not all of them did, he knew that. But he'd gotten burned out fast, disgusted by their complete lack of humanity. He didn't want to have this conversation at all, but definitely not in front of two virtual strangers. Too bad for him because it was clear that they weren't going anywhere.

Clearing his throat, he glanced away for a moment, unable to look at her as he searched for a way to get this out. Finally he looked back at her. "I never planned for this to be my job. Never imagined it actually. When I found out that Leo Williams was getting released on a technicality—that was the killer's name—I took care of the problem as soon as he was let out." And Axel felt no guilt over it either. The system had failed all the women Williams had raped, tortured and killed. It had failed in general. The system that should be protecting the marginalized had sat back and done nothing. That kind of apathy was just as bad as Williams killing people. "I couldn't let him continue—and he would have, no question. From there..." He shrugged, not going to give the whole story. Not yet anyway. And he'd only tell Hadley the rest if she wanted to know. But no one else.

Hadley was motionless and so were the others. The only exception was Skye who'd started eating, digging into an egg roll as if she hadn't eaten in a week.

"So, I'm going to process all that...later. For the issue at hand, why would anyone want to kidnap me?" Hadley asked, looking at everyone, pure confusion in her dark eyes.

Axel saw Skye and Brooks exchange a quick look as Skye set down her half-eaten egg roll on her plate.

Brooks took a step closer to his sister, his expression softening. He looked completely different from the man who'd been in the truck with Axel, ready to kill him. "Whether you want to accept it or not, you're wealthy. I know you won't take any money from Dad, but you're still considered a target because you're his daughter. And I'm going to be blunt. He adores you and he's not the same man who raised me. Don't get me wrong, when I was younger I was considered a target too and he took precautionary measures. It's part of the reason the ranch is so damn secure. He needed to know that wherever we lived, I was as safe as anyone could ever be."

"But why not go after you too? Not that I want you to be kidnapped," Hadley tacked on, her eyes growing wide. "I guess I just don't understand why me."

"Well he loves you and he's made it pretty damn clear to anyone who will listen. He's also incredibly proud of you. You're all he ever talks about now. And..." Brooks cleared his throat. "You're a woman, so they probably view you as an easier target. I have military training and there are other ways to use a woman against my father to get him to pay whatever it is this kidnapper wants."

It took a few seconds for Hadley to understand what her brother meant, but Axel saw the moment she did because her face paled. "That's...terrible."

Yeah, there were a lot of terrible people in the world. And Axel had taken out his share of them. The thought of anyone harming Hadley, using her as a pawn for money or whatever, made him see red.

"So have you guys called the police?" Hadley asked.

Skye snorted and Brooks simply shook his head.

"Why not?" She looked between the two of them, clearly avoiding Axel's gaze. He should probably just leave but he didn't want to be away from her. Not unless she explicitly told him to go.

"We're not going to involve the police for this," Brooks finally said. "Our crew is more capable of handling this kind of contract than some locals. We've got better technology, resources and we're not restricted by the law. And if we'd known about it a couple days ago,"

Brooks shot Axel a hard look, "we could have started digging more intensely."

"I've got a guy working on monitoring stuff," Axel said.

"Who are you using?" Skye asked.

It wasn't in his nature to share information but now was one of those times he had to. For Hadley's safety. When he said the guy's name, Skye nodded once. "Yeah, Isaac's all right. He's not Gage, but good enough."

"Who's Gage?"

"None of your fucking business," Brooks said. "I mean, ah, none of your business."

Hadley snorted. "You can say the F-word in front of me."

"So what were you planning on doing?" Skye asked Axel. "Were you planning on keeping Hadley safe while taking these guys out one by one? It's a pretty tall order when you're working alone."

Axel lifted a shoulder. "Pretty much. But you're right, I can't be in two places at once. I thought she'd be safe at the ranch."

"If you'd told someone, we could've kept her locked down," Brooks snapped, fire in his eyes now.

"Enough," Hadley muttered. "What do we do from here? Because school starts in a week and I'm not missing school. It was hard to get into this program and I won't let this jeopardize my career plan."

That might be too bad if they didn't figure out who had started this contract in the first place. But Axel didn't say that. He would let Brooks be the bad guy.

Brooks rubbed a hand over his face and sighed. "From this point forward, you'll stay at the ranch," he said to Hadley. "And we're going to figure out who hired someone to kidnap you and deal with him or her. That person is the real threat."

"What does 'deal with' mean?" she asked, though Axel figured she knew exactly what her brother meant.

Instead of answering, Skye gave a sort of feral grin and popped the last part of her egg roll into her mouth.

"Unless you have anything else to offer, you can leave now," Brooks said, his expression hard as he stared at Axel.

Axel nodded once. There was a lot he wanted to say to Hadley, but now wasn't the time. Still, he couldn't leave without saying something. "What I feel for you is real. I never meant to hurt you," he said quietly.

Surprising him, Hadley reached out and squeezed his hand once. Her expression was guarded but at least she didn't seem to hate him. A small victory.

Before she could say anything, Skye cleared her throat. "Seriously, O'Sullivan? That's pretty weak. You're gonna walk away after all this effort? You've already taken out two threats. You're coming with us to the ranch."

"Skye! What the hell is the matter with you?" Brooks demanded.

Skye gave him a hard look. "Last time I checked we were all cofounders and as far as I'm concerned this is officially a job. Plus...we all love Hadley too. Which means we all get to help with this and it's probably better if someone who isn't crazy emotional helps make decisions right now. And by someone, I mean you."

The two of them stared at each other in silence, as if they were having a telepathic conversation. Finally Brooks took Skye by the elbow and stepped into the attached laundry room, shutting the door behind them.

Which left Axel alone with Hadley. And she was still holding his hand. Seeming to realize that, she dropped it as if he was on fire and looked down at her lap.

The tension stretched between them, making him sick. He wished that he'd just come clean with her immediately. He wouldn't have gotten to know her if he had, but then maybe this wouldn't hurt so much either. Because the thought of walking away from her cut deep. "I'll go with you to the ranch if you want," he said quietly.

Her head popped up, her eyes widening slightly. "You don't have to do that. You've done more than enough for a stranger. And thank you for keeping me safe." Her cheeks flushed slightly and she looked away again, this time at a spot over his shoulder.

"I know I don't have to. I want to." He kept his voice low, wishing he could say everything he wanted to. That he'd started to fall hard for her, that he'd never meant to hurt her, that he'd do anything to keep her safe.

A few moments later, the other two stepped out of the laundry room, Skye looking pleased with herself and Brooks looking a little like he wanted to rip Axel's head off.

"If you want to join our crew for this job, we can use you." Brooks's expression was dark. "And the only reason I'm agreeing to this is because I've looked at your file and you're not a complete asshole. I know how you got started, and I can at least guess the rest of the details. Plus I know the rest of your background as well. You're not useless, and if you'd wanted to hurt or kidnap Hadley, you could have done it already. But you're on a short leash."

Axel simply nodded. He was a year older than Brooks, and while they hadn't worked any missions together, he knew the other man's reputation in the Marine Corps. And they'd both been honor grads—different graduation years.

"It's up to Hadley," Axel said quietly. "But yes, I want to be involved. I want to completely neutralize the threat to her. No matter what happens, I'll hand over all the information I have."

Hadley was silent for a long moment and just when he was convinced she was going to tell him to get the hell out, she gave him a surprisingly soft smile. "You can come to the ranch."

Tension eased from his shoulders but he simply nodded. He wasn't sure what to make of her wanting him there. It could mean absolutely nothing other than she simply wanted the extra protection. But the stupid part of him wished she wasn't completely disgusted by him and wanted him in her life. Maybe even wanted to finish what they'd started at the condo.

A man could hope.

CHAPTER ELEVEN

—Badass with a big heart.—

"So...how are you dealing with all this?" Skye asked quietly.

"You don't need to handle me with kid gloves." Hadley turned to stare at the window, watching the countryside pass in a blur of shapes, unsure how to answer that question. Because she had no idea how she was handling anything. It was a lot to process and she was slightly horrified with herself for not being more horrified about what Axel did for a living. Of course she wanted to talk to him more about it—in private—but wondered if he'd even tell her.

"I'm not trying to. But you just had a lot laid on you. Like the fact that the guy you may or may not be sleeping with is a hired killer. And that someone put out a contract to kidnap you. And you were attacked at school. That's a lot for anyone with training to deal with, let alone a civilian. It would be normal if you decided to freak out."

She softly snorted. "I'm not going to lose it." Not yet anyway. She might have a breakdown later when she was alone, but that wasn't normally how she handled things. She'd grown up keeping her feelings private, not letting anyone know her business. It was one attribute she'd gotten from her mom.

"Well I'm here if you need to talk."

"Will you share that file you have on Axel with me?" Because she wanted to know more about him.

"Sure, but he'll probably tell you anything you want to know."

"Yeah right," she muttered.

"Nah, he will. I can tell and I'm good at reading people." She said it so matter-of-factly.

Hmm. That gave her something to think about. "So why did you ask him to come to the ranch?" Because Brooks definitely didn't want him here but Skye hadn't seemed to care at all what her brother thought. The only reason Brooks had probably acquiesced was because he wanted to keep an eye on him and Darcy was at a condo instead of the main house. Her brother could be fiercely possessive of his fiancée—another reason she adored him.

"You want the truth?" Skye asked.

"Uh, yeah."

"Because he looks at you the way my husband looks at me. The way Brooks looks at Darcy. And the way Mercer looks at Mary Grace. He's not going to hurt you. And if we all get pulled in different directions with this whole operation, I like knowing that we have someone who will protect you with their life. Don't get me wrong, we would too, but he's not going to let you out of his sight. Not for anything. It's a logical decision to bring him in on this. Brooks is just being a protective older brother."

Wow. Okay, more stuff to digest. So much stuff. "Despite everything...I still kind of like Axel."

Skye nodded once. "I understand that. I know what he does for a living but...I'm definitely not judging."

Hadley started to respond when she saw a bundle of fur on the side of the road. "Stop!"

Instead of stopping immediately, Skye glanced in the rearview mirror, where Brooks and Axel were following them. She turned on her emergency blinkers and slowed before pulling onto the curb of the two-lane highway. They'd be at the ranch in about ten minutes and it was late enough that there weren't many people on the road.

"What's wrong?"

"I think I saw a dog back there. Or maybe a cat." Hadley was already unbuckling her seat belt, but Skye put a hand over hers.

"You stay put," the other woman said, pulling out her phone. She quickly texted Brooks, using voice to text.

A moment later Skye's phone buzzed. "Brooks is going to check it out. If it's an injured animal, we'll bring it back to the ranch."

All of her instincts told her to get out and help the animal, whatever it was. "I can go look—"

"Nope." Skye shook her head once for emphasis. "Look, if we're going to keep you safe, you have to listen to us. That means if we tell you to duck or get inside or whatever, you have to listen without asking questions." She glanced in the side mirrors, then the rearview.

Hadley knew that she was right because of this particular situation, but it was something she'd have to get used to. At least for the time being. "Okay."

Skye looked at her phone again after it buzzed. "It's a dog. They've got it."

"Is it injured? If so, what type of injuries? Do we need to take it to a vet?" There was a lot she could do on her own, but if it needed surgery they needed to get it help now.

Skye blinked once as she kicked the vehicle into gear. "That's literally the gist of what I know. It's a dog."

Rolling her eyes, Hadley pulled out her own phone. She thought about calling Axel, but in the end decided to simply text her brother with questions. She didn't have the energy to talk anymore, not to anyone.

She just hoped the dog was okay. Right now, she was going to focus on that and not Axel O'Sullivan or his haunted blue eyes, big callused hands and the groans he made when he came.

Nope, not thinking about any of that right now.

* * *

"What do you think we should name the dog?" Hadley asked as she finished brushing through the fur of the mixed-breed puppy. She guessed the puppy was part Shih Tzu and something else. "We need to call her something. At least until we find out if she has an owner or not," she added when Skye didn't respond.

At least the puppy hadn't been injured as far as she could tell. And she was also fairly young, maybe a year old, with good teeth. Hadley couldn't be sure about the age, but it was right around the time some people who had dogs decided that they weren't so cute anymore and got rid of them. Usually because they hadn't taken the time to train them correctly.

"I don't know," Skye said. "I don't know anything about dogs."

"Well she certainly likes you." Hadley ran a brush over the mutt's fur. It had taken an hour and a half to cut her filthy, matted fur off, then rinse her off and give her a thorough washing. And then she'd had to dry her—which the puppy hadn't liked—and now Hadley was simply brushing her short, soft fur.

But the puppy kept wiggling, making little whining noises as she looked at Skye who was sitting cross-legged against the opposite wall in the bathroom, watching the tiny ball of fur warily. "I don't know about that," Skye muttered.

"Oh yeah?" Hadley let go of the cute animal and she immediately raced at Skye, jumping into her lap and licking her face.

Skye scrunched her nose slightly but nuzzled the dog just the same. "At least you smell good now."

"I like the name Princess," Hadley said, mainly because they just needed to call her something.

"Gross. No." Skye shook her head.

"Okay, what name do you like?"

"I can't name this thing. Then it will never leave me alone," she said even as she started rubbing the dog's belly.

"Okay then how about Queenie?" Hadley held back her laughter, knowing that Skye would absolutely hate the name.

"Man, you stink at this. I'm going to call her C-4."

"Wait...what?"

"C-4. It's my favorite type of explosive."

Hadley started to laugh, but stopped when she realized Skye was serious. "You can't name a dog that."

"Why not?"

"Seriously?"

"You told me to name her." Skye pushed to her feet, taking the puppy with her. "Should we feed her or something? Is there even any food here?"

"Yeah, there's a bunch of dog stuff in one of the pantries here. I think my dad used to have a dog. Or maybe one of the ranch hands. We should also take her outside and see if she has to go to the bathroom."

Skye nodded and continued carrying the puppy, who was soaking up all the attention. Skye seemed to like the affection too, which Hadley found interesting. "I'll take her out back if you want to get some food ready?" Skye said as they reached the expansive kitchen.

"Sounds good." Hadley was really curious what her brother was doing with Axel and Gage—the hacker had shown up at the ranch right around the same time they'd arrived. She knew they must be going over whatever information Axel had, but she wished she was part of it. Brooks had sort of railroaded her and told her that he'd tell her everything later.

Which felt a lot like a lie. As if he was trying to appease her so he could only give her certain information. If someone wanted her kidnapped and whatever else, she had a right to know all the details. But she was still digesting everything about Axel and simply didn't have the energy to push back too hard against her brother.

She found dog bowls that were much too big for C-4—and holy crazy they couldn't actually name the dog that—and put a little puppy chow in one and water in the other. She even found a bed that was much too huge, but it would do for tonight. By the time she finished setting everything up, Skye strode back in, the puppy at her feet and her phone in her hand.

She half-smiled, clearly distracted when she saw Hadley. "C-4 did her business and I need to meet up with your brother. What room are you planning to stay in?"

"The one I always stay in." Brooks had made it clear that the room on the second floor he'd designated as hers was only hers. It was huge, nearly double the size of the room at her house, had a walk-in closet with clothes in her size and had clearly been professionally decorated. He'd recently added a framed photo of the two of them to one of the dressers.

"Oh, right. Okay. Then it wouldn't hurt for you to get some rest. You've had a long day."

"That's all you're gonna give me?"

"Sorry, hon." Skye scooped up the puppy. "There are some things I won't go over your brother on. He'll let you know what we've found in the morning, though, I promise." Hadley started to argue, but Skye added, "I'll text you later what room Axel is in."

"Why would I even care?"

Skye simply laughed. "You can do what you want with the information."

"Did you want me to keep the puppy?"

"Nah...I'll probably just take her bed into our bedroom." She motioned to the doggie bed Hadley had pulled out. "If she whines I just take her out to poop or whatever, right?"

"Yeah. Just let me know if you want me to take over. I don't mind."

"Nah, I think I've got this."

If that dog didn't have an owner, Hadley was pretty sure she'd just found one.

Hadley made her way to her bedroom, the one her father and Brooks had proudly showed her when they'd first invited her here. They'd been so adorable and nervous. Her dad didn't actually live in the main house—which Hadley was pretty certain would be considered a mansion—but on another smaller home on the property.

Which reminded her, she needed to call him. She was pretty certain Brooks had already told him everything so she wanted to check in with him. By the time she reached her room, her phone buzzed.

It was from Skye. *He's on the first floor in the room with the cowboy stuff. Northwest corner of the house.*

There was certainly no doubt who "he" referred to. And Hadley knew which room Skye was talking about too. She'd gotten the grand tour months ago and that room was pretty much on the opposite side of where hers was. Damn, Brooks wasn't messing around.

But...he also didn't get to tell her what to do. She made her own decisions, and the truth was, she wanted to see Axel. Wanted some answers. And maybe...something else. But she wasn't going to think about that now.

First, she needed a shower to wash the dog smell off her. Then, she was going to hunt Axel down. Whatever happened between them after that, happened.

CHAPTER TWELVE

—Old ways won't open new doors.—

Hadley stood in front of Axel's doorway for a long moment, contemplating the sanity of her decision. What the heck was she even doing here? Okay, who was she kidding? She knew exactly what she was doing.

She was drawn to him in a way she didn't completely understand, but she also wasn't going to fight it too much. Not until she heard more from him about his history. Because he'd held back at her place when talking to everyone. Now they'd be alone without her big brother to interfere.

Finally, she lifted her hand to knock lightly but the door swung open. She nearly stepped back at the sight of him, all broad-shouldered and ridiculously sexy. "Hey," she murmured, feeling awkward.

"I've been wondering how long it would take you to knock or if you were going to leave." His expression was neutral and she hated that.

She wrapped her arms around herself. "How did you know I was out here?"

He pointed down. "Saw the shadow of your feet. And I assumed it was you." He stepped back to let her enter.

Fighting the nerves dancing in her belly, she stepped into the nicely furnished bedroom, unsure exactly where to start.

"How's the dog?" he asked.

"She's good, and I'm pretty sure that Skye has officially adopted her. Or she will if we can't find her owner." Hadley still thought the dog's new name was ridiculous and hoped Skye changed her mind.

He simply nodded once and stood there looking slightly unsure of himself.

"Can we sit on the bed to talk?" She was feeling off-balance and she wanted to be as steady as possible. Sitting was better than standing.

"Oh yeah, of course." He stepped back and motioned toward the big king-size bed. A thick-looking quilt with little blue stars was slightly rumpled, but he hadn't pulled it back. And he was wearing lounge pants, a T-shirt and his laptop was open on the bed. So at least she hadn't interrupted his sleep.

Sitting down, she said, "I just came here to ask you some questions but don't feel obligated to answer anything."

He didn't sit on the bed next to her, but instead leaned against a nearby dresser. He reminded her of a caged lion as he crossed his arms over his broad chest, all the muscles in his forearms pulling tight. "Even if I know you won't like the answer, I'll be honest."

She pushed out a breath, trying to gather her thoughts. "Why did you come to see me in person? I mean, why come tell me in person, especially since you kind of know Brooks and you didn't know me at all."

He rubbed the back of his neck. "I'm honestly not sure I have an answer. You looked so sweet in the picture of the file I got on you. I just needed to tell you in person. I wanted to meet you," he muttered.

Oh. Well, that was certainly honest and she wasn't sure what to do with it. "But you didn't tell me. Instead you asked me on a date." To her surprise he looked down then and made a sort of grunting sound. So she pushed up from the bed and stood in front of him. "Why?" she pushed.

"Because I find myself fascinated by you," he murmured.

She wasn't sure why he was but she found herself fascinated by him too. "The feeling is mutual." Her voice was a whisper now. And when she swallowed hard, the sound felt overpronounced in the quiet room. "So why are you still here helping me?" she asked when he didn't respond.

"Because I want to see this through. I want to make sure you're safe."

"Do you feel like telling me how you ended up in your profession now? What happened after that first...job you did?" She was still trying to wrap her head around all of it.

He shoved out a breath. "I don't feel like telling you, but I will. Come on, let's sit together."

The sexual tension between them seemed to sky-rocket as she sat next to him on the edge of the bed. Being so close to him—on a big, welcoming bed—was messing with her senses.

"After I did what I did, I was feeling lost, I guess. I'd put out a few resumes, looking to do contract work overseas, and received a couple offers. Jobs with good pay and benefits. Then someone from my past reached out to me." He cleared his throat once. "Someone who was pretty sure I had killed Williams. Couldn't be certain, but this individual said that if I was looking for similar work, he had a job for me. And that it paid well. At first I balked, because there was no way I was getting into that kind of life. I knew he wasn't looking to set me up because..."

Axel cleared his throat.

"This guy lives in shades of gray. Then he sent me the contract. The contract was for a piece of human garbage who had slipped through the legal system a dozen times. Had killed at least eight people. I won't give you his list of crimes because they're revolting, but someone wanted him dead and they were willing to pay. So I took the job. Then I took another one, and another one. It got easier with each job. This individual, the one who sends me contracts, is sort of like my handler but not quite. He sends me jobs he knows I'll take. He's a facilitator, I guess you could call it. But what I do is illegal, there should be no doubt about that."

"Did he send you the contract on me?" she asked.

He nodded once, looking at her as he answered. "He sent it because he knew I would do something about it. He got it by mistake because you are *not* the kind of target we ever take." Silence stretched between them for a long moment.

She tried to think of something to say, for a way to respond, but kept coming up blank. How the heck could she even respond to that? Thanks for not...what? *Gah.*

Axel stood abruptly. "Look, I understand if you want me to just leave. I'm—"

"No, that's not what I want at all." She reached out and grabbed his hand on instinct, not even sure why she was doing it. *Liar, liar.* She wanted to touch him, simple as that.

He sat back down next to her, his expression slightly thawing. At least it wasn't completely neutral like before. Because she really hated that.

"I'm just trying to digest everything you told me. It's kind of a lot."

"I know. On top of all that, I know you're dealing with other stuff too. Like being attacked at your school. When I saw him hurt you, I lost it," he whispered. He reached up slowly, giving her time to push his hand away, and gently stroked a thumb over her throat, where her attacker had hurt her. His touch was feather soft and it sent little spirals of awareness curling through her until it all coalesced inside her belly.

She nodded slowly at his words, trying to get her brain to start functioning while he was touching her. She hadn't forgotten about the attack, but the truth was that it had taken a back burner since meeting Axel. Because it was impossible to think straight around him, especially when he was touching her so gently. "So…is this profession something you plan on doing forever?" Because she didn't think she'd be okay with that. No, she knew she wouldn't.

He shook his head as he dropped his hand. "I think I'm done."

"Seriously? Just like that?"

"If you ask me to quit, I will."

She blinked once. "I don't even know how to take that." They didn't even know each other. Why would he do that?

"There's not a lot you can ask me that I wouldn't do," he said softly, surprising her as he linked his fingers between hers.

Heat bloomed inside her, a volcano spreading out to all her nerve endings. Oh yeah, she'd completely lost her mind because she really didn't want to leave his room at all tonight.

"Do you think I could stay here with you tonight?" she whispered, feeling a little crazed and a lot turned on by him.

She was pretty sure she surprised him if the way he went completely still was any indication. She swore he even stopped breathing.

But he nodded and his eyes went molten hot.

* * *

Axel wasn't sure what Hadley was thinking, but he certainly wasn't going to tell her to leave. Not now, not ever. When she stared at him with those big brown eyes, with no recrimination—and he'd been so certain she'd hate him after he told her who he was and what he did for a living—he wanted to hold her close and never let go. But just because she wanted to stay the night with him didn't mean she wanted anything physical.

And he was okay with that. "Will you give me a few minutes?" he asked, rising from the bed. Because if he didn't put some distance between them, even for a few minutes, he was going to start kissing her senseless. And soon enough he'd be inside her.

She nodded, her cheeks all flushed and sexy as he headed to the bathroom. He wanted to brush his teeth and, okay, he needed space. To get his head on straight. There would be no sex tonight.

For reasons. Good ones. He just couldn't think of any that mattered when he knew that she was in his room, waiting on his bed. That soon he could have her spread out under him, his face between her legs.

He had to stop himself right there. By the time he got his body under control and stepped back into the room, he found her on his bed, his laptop on her lap.

She flushed when she saw him. "I saw the camera feeds of my house and got curious."

"You can use my computer for anything you want." His whole life was about secrets, but he didn't want to have any from her. "I was just scanning through the feeds to see if I missed anything."

"It's kind of weird that you had cameras at my place."

"Yeah, I know. And I'm sorry for violating your privacy."

"Considering why you did it...it's okay." She slid the laptop onto the bed next to her, so he took it and set it aside.

Then he slid in next to her and was surprised when she cuddled up next to him as if it was the most natural thing in the world. Hell, maybe she didn't want sex, so his "no sex" rule was a moot point anyway. She probably just didn't want to be alone. Not with everything going on.

Her entire life had been turned upside down and he could be a support for her. He wanted to be.

"Tell me more about your family," he said quietly, putting an arm around her, glad when she curled into him even more. He hadn't had a lot of peace in his life, but holding her like this soothed something inside him.

"Well, you know my mother died."

"Yeah."

"We had a very complicated relationship. If she was alive, I don't know how I would deal with the lies she told me."

"Lies?"

Hadley sighed softly. "I don't even know if she would consider them lies, but she told me that my dad was an asshole, that he wouldn't want me in his life. That he'd never gotten over his first wife, the one who died. That's Brooks's mom."

Axel was silent, just letting her talk.

"According to Brooks, and even according to my dad, he wasn't the best father to Brooks growing up. He wasn't abusive or anything, just kind of absent, drowning in his own pain. And that's between us," she added, shifting slightly so she could look up at him.

He nodded once. "Whatever you tell me stays between us."

She looked at him for a long moment, then continued as she laid her head back on his chest. "My mom moved us to the West Coast when I was really young. She was...oddly competitive with me. I didn't really understand it until I hit about fifteen. She was hypercritical of my appearance and now I can see that she simply hated getting older and took out her issues on me. She worked out four hours a day—yes, four—and was constantly worried about how she looked, what she ate or how many wrinkles she had. That kind of stuff, it never really mattered to me, probably because of her obsession with it. And the thing is, she was gorgeous. I mean, simply stunning."

Even if Axel hadn't done some digging on his own, he would have believed it because Hadley was too. It didn't matter what she wore, nothing could hide her beauty.

And even if it sounded cheesy in his own head, a lot of that had to do with who she was on the inside. She'd made them stop to save a dog on the side of the road when her own life was in danger. She always seemed to be thinking of others and he could admit that he was already addicted to her.

CHAPTER THIRTEEN

—Good things take time.—

Hadley wasn't sure what possessed her to open up so much to Axel, but she was just laying it all out there. If he could be honest about what he did for a living, she could be honest about where she came from and who her family was.

"My mom would do kind of weird stuff," she continued, cringing a little as she said all this out loud. "Like whenever I had friends over she tried to be their friend or flirt with boys from my class. Pretty gross stuff, if I want to be blunt. The overt flirting is why I stopped bringing people over finally. Honestly, I know kids have it way worse. My mom was dysfunctional, and…okay, she didn't really care if I had food to eat, but I think that had more to do with her viewing food as an enemy."

"Jesus," Axel muttered.

She let out a small, humorless laugh. "Yeah, it was kind of messed up, but I will say, the only thing she ever let me do was horseback riding. Once she saw how good I was, she wanted to put me in competitions and she actually paid for lessons and encouraged me in her own weird way. She kind of treated me like a show pony and she loved showing off how good I was to her friends, but

I didn't care because it was the one thing I loved." Hadley didn't think of her mom often. Or she tried not to. So it was weird to be talking about her now, but also kind of therapeutic.

He continued rubbing her back softly. Then he said, "So what's it like now that you have a family? A bigger family, I mean. One who seems to support you."

Pushing up, she sat next to him so she could look at him while they talked. Being cuddled up with Axel was heaven, but she liked looking into his blue eyes. "It's different. Especially since all of Brooks's friends treat me like a little sister. I really like it. Actually, I love it, but I found that I have to draw some boundaries with them because they seem to think I'm fifteen and not twenty-two."

"Twenty-two," he muttered.

She pinched his side. "You've always known how old I am."

"Yeah, but it makes me feel ancient right now."

Axel took one of her hands in his, linked his fingers through hers, and she melted a little more.

"So, tell me about your mom," she said. "You only said that you guys weren't close."

His expression went carefully neutral so she decided to lay her head back on his chest, sensing that looking into his eyes made it harder for him. He shifted, wrapping his arm around her again, and she just wanted to burrow into him. She hoped it would be easier for him to talk with her lying this way, without feeling like he was being scrutinized.

"You don't have to tell me anything," she murmured, resting one hand on his chest. Even if she was really curious. Because she wanted to know everything about this man, everything that made him tick. He'd already opened up to her in such a huge way, she wouldn't push anymore. Not tonight anyway.

He slid his hand down along her side and hip until his big hand was more or less grazing the top of her butt. Holy hell, that shouldn't get her worked up, but it made her wonder if he planned to do anything else or if cuddling was the only thing on the menu for tonight. Some of her friends from school would have no problem making the first move, but she wasn't feeling brave right now. After the other night, after the way she'd stroked him off, she wanted him to make the move this time.

His fingers flexed once against her hip, sending a rush of heat through her. The man was huge all over. She could clearly see the outline of his erection, but he seemed content to simply lie there with her.

"I want to tell you about my past too. I have no idea who my father was, and honestly, I don't think my mom knew either. She was sort of like your mom, I guess, trying to recapture her youth, or just hold on to it. She liked to party and she didn't mind leaving me home alone. If it hadn't been for a neighbor, I wouldn't have eaten most nights. We lived in this shitty little trailer, so I was what you would consider white trash. I didn't really understand that until I hit middle school."

He was silent for a long moment and she gently kissed his chest, hating the thought of him going hungry. He was quiet for a while and she thought he might be done.

"She partied too hard one night and went home with the wrong man," he finally said. "The guy killed her." His voice was completely devoid of emotion.

Stunned, Hadley pushed up so she could look at him. "Axel, I'm so sorry."

He lifted a shoulder, the sheets rustling with the movement. "It was a long time ago. I was sixteen then. So I was put in the system for a couple years, and got pretty lucky. I only lived with two families, and they weren't great but they also weren't abusive. I think it's because of my size. They pretty much left me alone, cashed their checks, and I got to finish school in the same school district I'd lived in with my mom. Trust me, I've seen a hell of a lot worse."

She was sure that he had, given that he'd worked for the FBI. Shifting up closer, she brushed her lips over his, only intending a chaste kiss, but he immediately deepened it, his tongue teasing her mouth open in the most dominating, possessive way.

And she melted into him, unable to resist this sexy, wonderful man who'd come to Redemption Harbor simply to protect her because of a file he'd read. She was coming to terms with what he did for a living, but she still wanted him.

Desperately. And she wasn't sure what that said about her.

She started to climb onto him, straddling him, but found herself flat on her back underneath him instead. He made a sort of sexy growling sound as he plundered her mouth, his huge erection pressed against her belly.

Heat flooded between her thighs as she thought about what he would feel like pressing into her. She'd already heard him come, knew how intoxicating it was to see and hear a man like Axel lose control, and she wanted him to do it with her now. Wanted to know him in the most intimate way possible.

"Want to taste all of you," Axel murmured against her lips, his voice thrilling. And his words?

She was about to combust from them. Hadley thought she said okay or tried to get an answer out even if he wasn't really asking anything. But it came out as more of a strangled moan as he started lifting her shirt up, up, up.

She hadn't bothered with a bra after her shower and now she was really, really grateful when his hands skimmed her bare breasts.

And froze.

Maybe he'd been expecting her to have one on. He only paused for a moment before he cupped them fully, teasing her already hard nipples as he continued kissing

her. His assault on her mouth was delicious and overwhelming and she felt as if she'd never been truly
kissed before. Or at least she'd never been kissed by
someone like Axel.

Demanding and intense and so sexy he lit her on
fire.

In another couple seconds her sweater was off and
he was looking down at her as if she was the most
beautiful woman in the world. As if she was the only
thing that mattered. It was impossible not to be affected.

"I want to make you come." The words came out
as a growl, but also a question.

Oh yeah, she was here for this. All night long. She
nodded because she didn't trust her voice.

Keeping his gaze pinned to hers, he slowly started
tugging her pants down her legs, hooking his fingers
into her panties as he went, pulling everything off at
once. The house was heated and the room was perfectly comfortable, but being fully exposed to Axel
like this now made her feel vulnerable.

Which wasn't necessarily a bad thing, but it was
hard not to feel self-conscious as his scorching gaze
swept over her from head to toe. Kneeling in between
her spread legs, he said, "You're so perfect."

Just like that, all the tension inside her dissipated.
She started to reach for him when he covered her

body with his again. She arched into him, her sensitive breasts rubbing against the soft fabric of his shirt and hard muscle beneath.

When he reached between their bodies, gently cupping her mound, she moaned into his mouth. Slowly, he began teasing between her already slick folds, his movements unhurried and sensual.

As he slid a finger inside her, she bit his bottom lip harder than she'd intended. He liked it, if the sexy growl he made and the way he rolled his hips against her was any indication.

"Want to taste your come," he whispered, a hint of wicked in his clear blue eyes as he started kissing a path across her chest, pausing at one breast.

He sucked a nipple into his mouth even as her brain was computing his words. Her past lover, as in singular, had been a college boyfriend. Everything had been rushed, and in hindsight, she realized it had been all about him. Now...she arched off the bed as Axel lightly pressed his teeth around her hardened nipple. It was all about her.

There was no pain, just the hint of it, which made her pleasure that much more pronounced. Combined with the way he was stroking inside her, all her nerve endings felt as if they were on overload.

It wasn't going to take much to make her come. Not when he was playing her body so expertly. As he alternated between her breasts, teasing, kissing, and gently nipping, he kept stroking her, over and over.

Her inner walls tightened more and more with each stroke, as she pushed closer to the edge of release. Oh God, this felt so good. Too good. She could barely think and breathe as her muscles tightened convulsively around him.

The path he kissed down her stomach tingled with each kiss, as if he was marking her, claiming her. Maybe that was her imagination and right now she didn't care.

She was so damn close.

By the time he knelt between her spread thighs, her legs were trembling. And when his tongue teased her clit, she nearly vaulted off the bed. At first he was gentle and soft, but he increased his pressure even as his strokes remained steady.

She dug her fingers into his short hair, holding on to him as he brought her so much pleasure she could hardly stand it. "Axel." When she moaned out his name, he made a sexy growling sound, which reverberated through her clit.

Too. Much.

She didn't just fall, she catapulted over the edge as pleasure shot out to her nerve endings, her clit pulsing with each stroke from his wicked, wicked tongue. Not feeling vulnerable anymore, she rolled her hips against his face as her orgasm punched through her, until she collapsed against the soft bed, a mass of nerves. Her breathing was erratic as she looked down her body at him.

His blue eyes were bright with hunger. For her.

She reached for him, wanting to feel him inside her. More than just his fingers. All of him. Every delicious inch.

He slid up her body, covering her again as she wrapped her legs around him.

"That was incredible," she murmured.

He brushed his lips over hers once as he slid a hand down to grip her hip, his fingers flexing against her bare skin. The hold was possessive and gentle at the same time.

When she reached between their bodies, he stilled. "I...don't have a condom."

She didn't either, but... "I'm on the pill. And I'm clean."

"I am too but...I think we should wait." He didn't move off her and the lust in his eyes didn't dim, but the set of his jaw was firm.

"Why?"

"I want to make sure you're really ready for this. You've been through a lot recently. Hell, you're still dealing with a lot. I...don't want to be someone you regret."

Her eyes widened at his words, at the raw vulnerability that sparked in his gaze. "I won't regret this." Of that she had no doubt.

He kissed her again, this time deeper, hungrier. "I...still want to wait."

Sighing, she simply ran her fingers down his still-covered back. She really wished he was naked, but wasn't going to push. Much. "So...how long do we have to wait?"

He let out a startled laugh before kissing her again.

And he didn't actually answer. But that was okay. She had a feeling his control was razor thin now, especially given the erection she felt against her belly. If he was only worried about her having regrets, he didn't need to.

Soon enough, she'd make sure he understood that.

CHAPTER FOURTEEN

—The queen of awkward.—

Hadley eased the door to Axel's bedroom open since he was still in the shower. She'd told him that she was headed back to her room to do the same, and even though he'd asked her to join him, she needed to clear her head a little bit. Especially since he was still all about his "no sex right now" thing. Getting into a shower with him while they were both naked? No, not good for her sanity.

As she stepped into the hallway, she froze when she saw her dad standing there, eyes wide.

Well, talk about awkward. Brooks had told her that he'd be coming back to Redemption Harbor a week early but he didn't live in the main house and, well, she hadn't expected him quite so early in the morning. Definitely not to be standing right outside Axel's door.

"Hey, Dad," she murmured and inwardly cursed when she felt her cheeks flush.

"Well, I was coming to talk to the man who saved you." His voice was dry.

"He's in the shower." Yep, she was definitely the queen of making things even more awkward.

Her dad looked lost for a moment as he stood there so she stepped forward and gave him a hug. "I'm glad to see you."

He frowned as he stepped back. "I would've come home sooner if I'd known about that mugging." There was a little chastisement in his voice. "Which sounds like it wasn't a mugging at all," he added.

Yeah, she should have told him. But to be fair, she wasn't used to having family, to having people to check in with. This was all new to her. Even reaching out to Mary Grace the other night had been out of character for her. She was so used to simply handling things on her own. Since she didn't want to stand around outside Axel's door she said, "I could really use some coffee right about now."

Her dad's expression eased, his handsome face becoming even more so as he smiled. And not for the first time she thought that he and Brooks could have been movie stars. He slung an arm around her shoulders as he headed down the hallway. "I missed you," he said. "And no matter what, we're going to do everything we can to figure out who put that contract out on you." It was subtle, but she heard a hint of anger in his voice now.

"We?"

"Well, Brooks and his guys will do what they do, but I'll be staying here in the main house and we ramped up security around the ranch as well. So... What's going on with you and Axel O'Sullivan?"

Gah, what did he want to know exactly? This was new territory for her and she wasn't sure how to answer so she evaded for the moment. "Do you know him or did Brooks tell you about him?"

"Brooks told me about him and I also read the file your brother gave me on the guy," he said as they stepped into the expansive kitchen. Her dad immediately went for the Bunn coffee maker so she let him start a pot as she sat at the island. The granite-topped island was a lot bigger and a lot fancier than the small one at her house. It could probably seat up to twelve people comfortably. And the huge table by the window could also seat as many. It was still hard to wrap her mind around the fact that Douglas Alexander was her father. She'd always known he was, but the knowledge had been abstract. Being here, on his ranch, really drove home the differences in their lifestyles.

"Is there anything else you want to say about him?" she asked when he didn't continue.

Her dad gave her a small smile as he glanced over his shoulder. "I'll be having a talk with him later."

That sounded ominous, but she hadn't had any caffeine and Axel was a grown man who could handle himself so she simply nodded. "Okay."

"So tell me how you're doing, really. You were attacked at your school and now someone wants to kidnap you. That's pretty heavy stuff to deal with." He slid a now full mug of coffee across the island countertop and sat in front of her. When she started to get up he waved his hand once. "You sit. I'll get the creamer and sugar. I know what you like."

She grinned as he did just that. According to Brooks, this was an entirely new side to their dad and she could admit that she was glad she'd only ever seen this side of him. This was the kind of father she'd always imagined having.

"Well honestly, I'm not sure how I'm dealing with it. It feels kind of surreal, like it happened to someone else. I still can't believe someone wants to kidnap me. It's too crazy."

Her dad lifted a shoulder as he set the creamer and sugar in front of her. "It's not so crazy, considering I'm your father. And not to bother you about this again, but once this mess is over—and it will be over soon—I hope you reconsider letting me get you a place with better security. It doesn't have to be anything fancy, but I'd sleep better at night knowing you had more security protocols in place. I want to make sure you're safe and protected." His expression was so serious and worried as he stood across the counter, his own coffee cup in hand.

Her instinct was to say no, but considering what was going on she realized that no matter what she wanted, her life circumstances had changed. And just because she wasn't actually wealthy clearly didn't mean that anyone who wanted to get to her father would understand that. And she didn't want to go through this again. "I'll think about it."

His dark eyebrows rose. "Well, it's not a no."

She grinned. "Nope, it is not. So how did your trip go? And how is Martina?"

Her dad gave a soft smile at the mention of Martina, the woman he was currently dating. Martina was also Nana to Valencia, Olivia's daughter. Olivia was a security specialist who broke into places and showed the owners their weaknesses. And right now she was on her honeymoon with her new husband, Zac Savage. Hadley had gotten to know all of them over the last couple months and especially adored sweet Valencia. The little girl was full of fire and life.

"With everything going on, I put up Martina and Valencia in one of my condos. They're right next to the place Darcy is staying in. It's got great security, and with Olivia and Savage being out of town I wanted to make sure they were in the most secure place possible. It's unlikely that Martina is a target but since she's taking care of Valencia, and because I love her, we're taking extra precautions. They've got a couple security guys staying with them as well as the guys who are watching Darcy, so they're locked down tight."

"Did you just say you're in love with Martina?"

Her dad's cheeks flushed the faintest shade of pink as he lifted a shoulder. "Yeah. For the first time since Brooks's mom, I'm...in love. It feels weird."

"How did you know you were in love the first time?" she asked quietly. Because she'd never been in love and she was pretty certain she was edging into that territory with Axel. Whether or not it was smart or sane was a completely different story. Because her heart was all about Axel.

Her dad's eyes widened and he got a slightly panicked look. "Are you asking for any particular reason?"

Her brother chose that moment to step into the kitchen. He smiled when he saw the two of them, and Hadley was thankful when her dad didn't say anything else about the question she'd just asked. It was one thing to ask her dad about being in love but another entirely to talk to Brooks about it.

Her brother immediately stepped toward her and wrapped an arm around her shoulders, squeezing her once before he kissed her on the top of her head. "You better have saved some coffee for me."

"Nope, I drank it all."

Snickering slightly, he headed toward the coffee maker and poured himself a mug.

"So how's Darcy doing? And how are you doing being separated from her?" Hadley hated that Darcy wasn't here, that she was staying at some condo because of all this.

"She's good." He snorted once. "She loves the condo, said she could get used to all the perks it's got."

"Really? So she's not mad about...not being in her own home?"

Brooks blinked once. "She's not mad at all. It's actually easier for her to stay in the condo now. She just took on a couple new clients she met at the wedding expo and they live downtown—and almost all of her business contacts are downtown. I've got security on her and we're not taking any chances. If I thought she was in danger, she'd be here under lock and key."

"You're sure?"

"Yeah. This threat isn't about her, or me. It's about..." He glanced at their dad. "It's about him. Someone wants to hurt him, and to do that, you're the smartest option. I think Gage made some progress last night and we have an idea to bait one of the men sent to kidnap you."

Her heart skipped a beat. "One of? I thought there was only one left."

He nodded once. "Yeah that's what Axel said, and if his intel is good, then it is just one. But I don't like to take anything at face value. Besides, he might not know everything. There could be others out there we don't know about."

Suddenly the coffee in her stomach turned sour. She'd known this was a possibility, but she'd been clinging to the hope of what Axel had told them about the three men being sent after her. Two of them weren't a problem anymore.

"We're going to figure out who hired these guys in the first place," her dad said, his expression harsh. In that moment she saw a flash of the brutal businessman he must be.

Next to him Brooks nodded in agreement. The two of them looked so much alike there was no denying they were related. Both tall, classic good looks, dark hair and dark eyes. She was glad that she'd gotten the trademark Alexander dimple. It made her feel more like part of the family.

"What's wrong? I mean other than the obvious?" Brooks asked, his frown deepening.

She shook her head. "Nothing... I was actually just thinking about how glad I am to have you two in my life."

Just like that the two men seemed to melt right in front of her. Her dad nudged Brooks once. "She's considering moving to a place with better security after this whole mess is dealt with."

"Good." Brooks nodded once in approval. "And don't you doubt that it will indeed be taken care of. That's actually why I'm down here. As soon as you're ready I want to meet in my office and go over some things with you."

She knew this was really going to bother Brooks but she wasn't going to leave Axel out of anything. Not after last night. "So, you're probably going to be annoyed with me, but are you going to ask Axel to join us as well?"

His jaw clenched once. "I guess."

"Seriously? You guess? He didn't have to come and warn me. He doesn't have to be here right now. And from what I understand he wanted to pay off that second guy who was sent after me. With his own money."

Brooks just stood there like a statue for a long moment with what she was sure was supposed to be an intimidating expression, but it was hard to be scared of him. At least for her. Finally he spoke. "I can concede that he's done some good things. But I don't have to like everything about him and I don't have to like the fact that he's interested in you."

"Well I'm inter—"

Her dad cleared his throat. "Hadley, why don't you go grab a shower and I'll get breakfast started."

If that wasn't a dismissal, she wasn't sure what was. Instead of telling Brooks how she felt about Axel, she picked up her mug and kissed both men on the cheek before heading to her room. She'd let her dad and Brooks hash out whatever they needed to hash out. It wasn't going to change the fact that she was seriously into Axel and that wasn't changing anytime soon. He'd laid himself bare to her and she accepted him for who he was.

She just wondered what she was to him. It was pretty clear that he was attracted to her, even if he was holding off on sex. Frustrating man.

For now, she just wanted to take a shower, check her school email, and think about what she and Axel had shared not too long ago. He'd brought her to orgasm again in the middle of the night and she'd stroked him off again. Next time she wanted to taste him...and she really needed to stop thinking about that or she was going to get herself all worked up again.

CHAPTER FIFTEEN

—I won't be impressed with technology until I can
download snacks.—

Hadley stood next to Axel, making him secure in a
way he hadn't realized he'd needed as they all stood
in Brooks's office. He hadn't been sure how she'd act this
morning in front of the others and he'd been preparing
for her rejection.

After what they'd shared last night, he was pretty
damn certain he wanted to eventually put a ring on her
finger. Not now—it was too soon and she could decide
he wasn't worth the trouble. But if she decided he wasn't
someone she'd regret, then...one day. Probably sooner
than later. Which, hell. He had to stop getting ahead of
himself. It was damn hard when he had this newfound
hope.

So when he'd stepped into the office with Brooks,
Colt and Skye, and Gage, an apparent hacker, Axel had
been inordinately pleased when she'd walked right up to
him and brushed her mouth over his. He'd actually fro-
zen for a moment, unsure how to react. Now she stood
next to him, her fingers loosely linked between his,
clearly making a statement to everyone in the room.

He might not deserve her, but he certainly wasn't going to walk away from her. Not ever. Unless she told him to.

"This would be a whole lot easier if we were at the office because I could show you on bigger screens." Gage sat behind the huge desk, working on his laptop as they all waited for him to pull up whatever he was pulling up. "But we're going to make do with what we've got here. Okay, I dumped the contents of the phone you gave me," he said, flicking a quick glance at Axel. "There wasn't much on there. It was definitely a burner phone but I'm still running information on all the phone calls Johnson made. He thought he deleted everything but luckily I'm smarter than a phone. Next, the cameras you set up are good. If I'd set them up myself, I would have picked the same angles."

Hadley gently squeezed Axel's fingers and Brooks simply gave him an annoyed look. Oh yeah, it was going to take a hell of a lot to get Brooks to forgive him.

"I've been monitoring them and so far nothing seems out of the ordinary," Gage continued. "Except for this. And it might not even be anything." He paused for a moment as he fast-forwarded to an image, then pressed play. A four-door sedan with tinted windows drove by at a normal speed once. Then he fast-forwarded to another clip. It was the same vehicle driving by at a slow speed, at a different time of day, given the angle of the shadows.

"I ran the plate on his vehicle and it didn't come back in the system. Which could mean any number of things but my guess is the plate doesn't exist."

"How can it not exist?" Hadley asked.

Gage didn't look up from the computer as he answered. "More than likely someone welded two license plates together, creating a number that isn't registered."

"That's pretty smart," Hadley murmured.

Gage shrugged. "Eh. It's Criminal Behavior 101. Anyway, since I can't figure out where the plate is from and the car is generic enough that I can't do much with it, my guess is this might be the guy we're looking for. Or it could be something completely unrelated, but I don't believe in coincidence."

"So what do we do with this information?" Hadley asked.

"That's where I come in," Skye said. "I'm going to be the bait and head back to your place, pretend to be you. See if we can pull this guy out of hiding and get him to make a move."

Next to Axel, Hadley stiffened. "I don't like the sound of that. I don't want anyone getting hurt because of me."

Skye snorted. "The only person getting hurt is the guy who thinks he can kidnap you. Trust me. I'm not going alone anyway. Colt is coming with me. I'm going to wear a disguise, making it look as if I'm you to a casual observer. And I'll drive your car back to your place. Then inside the garage Colt will get out of the back seat and we'll set up camp at your place. And Brooks is going to be nearby as backup if we need him."

Hadley nodded but it was clear she didn't like the idea of any of this. "What about me? What am I going to do?" she finally asked.

"You're going to stay here where we know you're safe. And Axel is going to be your shadow," Skye said.

Brooks simply gave him another hard stare. But Axel nodded and gave her an encouraging smile. He hadn't planned to leave her side anyway.

Her cheeks flushed that sexy shade of pink and she squeezed his fingers but didn't say anything else.

Axel didn't like staying out of the action because he wanted to be the one to bring this guy down, but he wanted to protect Hadley a whole lot more. And he wanted to be the one by her side. He might not be able to control everything, but he could sure as hell keep her safe. More than anything, she was the priority. "Have you found anything on the person who actually hired these guys?" he asked.

"I'm working on it," Gage said. "Douglas has already pulled up all of his old and recent business deals to see if there's someone he might have pissed off. Because this feels personal. Kidnapping his daughter, the daughter he just found out about, with the intention of—" Gage glanced at Hadley then cleared his throat. "Anyway, I'm working hard on that angle and following the money trail of anyone who's a suspect. But nothing solid as of yet."

Axel nodded. That would have to be good enough for now. And he agreed with the other man because this did feel personal. "I can do grunt work if you need extra eyes on your files or whatever." He'd worked for the Feds once so he understood how tedious that kind of work could be.

"All right, thanks. I'll let you know."

That would have to do for now.

* * *

"So what do you think of Axel?" Skye asked as she and Colt stepped inside Hadley's cute little home. The way she'd decorated was homey, with earth tones. It reminded her a little of Darcy's place. Soft, sweet women that Skye was a little baffled to be friends with.

He moved to the security panel and punched in her code. "She needs a better system. Actually, she needs to move somewhere more secure in general."

"Yeah, I know. After this I bet she will." Even if Hadley didn't like the idea of her dad paying for a place for her, it was only logical that she move somewhere different after this. A condo with a doorman and security. And she needed freaking cameras too. Not this basic security system that a toddler could hack.

Colt set his bag of weapons on the center island. "To answer your other question, he seems okay. His file from the FBI is solid. And even the jobs he did—or the ones we suspect him of doing—I won't be losing any sleep about the assholes he took out."

"I was thinking more along the lines of what do you think of recruiting him?" She'd thought that had been clear.

But Skye realized she'd surprised her husband as he paused. "You're serious?"

"We've been taking on more jobs and everyone has family and might not be able to take last-minute jobs. It wouldn't hurt to have more employees. Since we can't do actual interviews for the stuff we do, and he clearly works in a gray area already...he's kind of perfect for the type of person we're looking for. I'm not saying definitely, because we don't know enough about him yet, but I see the way he looks at Hadley. He's not going anywhere."

Colt nodded at that. "Yeah, he looks at her like Gage looks at his computers."

She snickered. More like how Gage looked at Nova, their office manager/woman-who-kept-them-all-in-line. Something neither of them would say aloud, not when Gage was currently on their comm line. "It'll drive Brooks nuts."

Colt shrugged. "If things work out with those two, he'll get over it."

True enough. Now it was time to get to work. "So how do you want to do this?"

He glanced around the small, clean kitchen. "I'll head upstairs and set up while you stay down here.

We can open a few blinds as if they got left open by accident and you can turn the TV on. If you sit at the right angle, it'll look like Hadley. Whoever is after her only has pictures of her. They won't know her well enough to know it's not her."

Skye patted her wig once. She'd learned the art of disguises when she'd been with the CIA, so slipping into this role had been easy. "Sounds like a plan to me. Should we leave the alarm system on or off?"

He paused for a moment. "Off."

She nodded once. "Yeah, that's what I was thinking." They didn't want an alert going out to Hadley's security company. If someone did break into Hadley's house, Skye was certain they could neutralize any threat quickly and efficiently, but it was better not to take any chances. Because they didn't plan on involving law enforcement in anything.

"Did you get all that?" Skye asked into her earpiece.

"Yep," Gage said. "And not that you guys asked for my opinion, but I agree about Axel. I kinda like the guy."

Skye grinned at her husband. She had a good sense about these things and Colt was a great judge of character. Since her husband hadn't said no outright, she figured that he must feel the same way about the man as well.

Before they did anything else, Skye leaned over and pressed her mouth to Colt's. Hard and fast. "A kiss for good luck."

Her husband grinned at her as he opened up one of their duffel bags and pulled out a SIG. Her favorite.

Taking the weapon, she tucked it into her holster and kept it hidden. It was showtime.

CHAPTER SIXTEEN

—Love is a lot of things, but it should never be hard.—

He drove down his target's street at a normal speed, not wanting to draw any undue attention. For the first time in the last twenty-four hours, he spotted lights on downstairs. Time to get to work.

Instead of parking on her street, he headed down a couple blocks and parked near a children's park. It should be easy enough to subdue her, then grab his vehicle and dump her in it. Or he would just toss her in the trunk of her own car, which was no doubt in the garage. It was early enough so she should be eating dinner or doing homework or whatever college-aged girls did. He didn't know and didn't care. All he knew was that he was going to get paid. The guy who'd hired him seemed like a jackass, but his money was good and that was all that mattered. Because jackasses made the world go round.

As he headed toward her house, there was a woman walking her dog about thirty yards in front of him on the sidewalk so he crossed to the other side. He'd worn jogging gear, a beanie and a headset—that wasn't pumping out any music. But he needed to blend in, play the part. It wasn't so late that jogging was out of the ordinary so the woman might remember seeing some guy out, but she wouldn't remember him. Out of the corner of his eye he watched her as her dog took a crap.

She didn't even look over in his direction. Perfect. Keeping his pace steady, he headed down the street then looped back around. The woman and her dog were gone.

The time was right that most families would be having dinner with their kids or spouses. It was a Sunday so people were winding down from the weekend and getting ready to head back to work tomorrow. He might not have a typical job but he understood people and their routines.

Her neighbors didn't seem to have outdoor dogs either so that was a plus. From his file on the female, he had her address, marital status—single—and other benign information. The only thing not benign was who her family was. Her father, specifically. Some rich douche. He figured the man could have sprung for better digs for his kid but that wasn't his problem. Besides, this place was in a "safe" neighborhood. She probably felt safe right now.

Instead of heading for the front porch, he ducked around the side of the house. Damn. She didn't even have security lights. As he crept up to the nearest window, he kept his back against the wall. There was a sign for a security system out front, but in his experience that didn't always mean there was one. And the system she had was generic enough. Besides, if he held a gun to her head, he was pretty much guaranteed she'd turn the system off anyway. People were often predictable.

After a quick scan around the side of her small yard and her neighbor's house, he saw that he was alone so he turned and peered through the windows. Blinds covered them, but one was slightly pushed up. Looking inside, he saw the profile of a woman sitting on a cream-colored couch. Her legs were kicked up on a tufted storage bench. The television was on some kind of nature show.

He couldn't get a clear shot of the woman's face. But the hair was the right color and this was the target's house so it was a pretty good chance it was her. Next to her was a glass of water on the side table.

Her marital status was single but the guy who'd hired him hadn't known if she was dating anyone. If she was, the guy wasn't here. Didn't mean he couldn't show up, if he existed at all.

Frowning, he watched her for a few moments. She flipped the channel a few times during a commercial, but ended up back on the same nature show. Then she took a sip of her water. Then more TV watching.

Pretty boring shit. As he contemplated making a grab for her now, waiting until it was about three or so in the morning, or setting up cameras to watch her for a few days, he realized that her shoes were still on.

He wasn't sure why it struck him as wrong but it did for some reason. She wore a simple sweater and jeans.

And her shoes were kicked up on the bench. When people came home they took off their shoes, sweaters, scarves. It was one of those human nature things.

It probably meant nothing and he was almost certainly being paranoid, but he still didn't like it. He also noticed that she didn't have a cell phone with her. Or if she did, she wasn't checking it. He'd read that people checked their phones something like eighty times a day. Hell, that was probably an understatement.

Since he hadn't had enough time to do much recon on this place, he decided to ease off for now. He hadn't remained alive and in business for so long by getting sloppy. Yes, he wanted to get paid, but he wasn't going to get stupid.

Easing away from the window, he started back the way he'd come. But before he left, he stopped by a tree facing her place from a perfect angle. He'd have a great shot of her front door and garage.

Pulling one of his cameras out, he started to quickly install it when he saw another camera in the bark. *Holy. Shit.* It might be one of the other people who'd been hired, it could be her own security camera or it could be something else altogether. Either way he definitely didn't like it.

His internal radar pinged, telling him to get the hell out of there. Now.

Without missing a beat, he pocketed his camera and stepped onto the sidewalk. As he headed down the street, he glanced around to see if he was being watched. There were vehicles in driveways, and some driveways were empty so it was impossible to tell if anyone was inside. His radar was definitely going off, but that could be because he'd found the camera and not because someone was actually watching him.

As he reached the end of the street, he took a right and picked up his pace, breaking into a light jog. He'd have to double back to where he parked his vehicle, then ditch it. The precaution was worth it because if someone tried to tail him, he'd notice. He wasn't going to bail on the job completely, but he was definitely going to do more recon on this target before he went in.

* * *

"He's leaving," Gage said.

"You're sure?" she asked, pushing up from the couch as she adjusted her earpiece.

"Yes. He saw one of the cameras. He was trying to set up one of his own. I got a great shot of his face." Gage sounded gleeful and Skye could practically see him rubbing his hands together like a cartoon villain.

Skye cursed under her breath even as Colt met her at the bottom of the stairs. "We'll tail him."

"I'll start the tail," Brooks said along the comm line.

"When did you show up?" He'd told them he was going to stop by the condo where Darcy was staying to spend a little time with his fiancée.

"About an hour ago. Didn't want to bother you on the comm. But I managed to put a tracker on his vehicle," Brooks added. "He parked at the children's park not too far away."

"He'll probably ditch the thing as soon as he can." At least that was what Skye would do. He wouldn't have time to scan the car for electronics, and if the guy had half a brain, he would have a backup plan in place. And said backup plan should include a different getaway vehicle. Of course the guy could be a complete dumbass and lead them straight to wherever he was holed up.

"Keep an eye on her place." The temperature dropped by about ten degrees as Skye and Colt stepped into the garage. Mother Nature seriously needed to get her shit together this year.

Gage simply snorted in her ear, his only response. Because of course he would. She was so used to giving orders, however, that sometimes she said the obvious.

Skye slid on her gloves and held her hand out for the keys but Colt shook his head, grinning.

"It's my turn to drive." His breath curled in front of him like a wisp of faint, white smoke.

"I'm a better driver," she said even as she rounded to the other side.

"Please." Colt slid into the driver's seat as she did the same on the passenger side.

"You really want to debate who's a better driver?"

"There is no debate."

"Exactly. Because I am clearly superior." She sniffed slightly.

"You two both suck at driving," Brooks muttered. "If there's a contest for who's the crazier driver, Skye, you would definitely win. But Colt comes in second... I'm taking a turn onto Ward Street. Looks like he's headed south."

"He's likely heading out of the residential area and toward one of the more industrial districts," Colt said.

Skye wasn't from Redemption Harbor, unlike her husband, Brooks and the rest of the team. But she'd studied the city since moving here and knew what area he was talking about. "So how's Darcy doing?" Skye asked Brooks.

"Sitting tight at the condo. She's busy with her new clients and barely noticed I was there."

Well that was surely a lie. "I got a look at some of the security guys at her condo and they're quite muscled. And good-looking," Skye murmured.

Colt shot her a hard look as she contained a laugh. She mouthed *I'm kidding*, but his expression didn't soften. She'd make it up to him later.

"Seriously? You're messing with me now?" Brooks muttered.

"Come on, I've gotta have some fun. We're headed south on Ivy Lane right now. I can see you up ahead but we'll hang back out of sight." She steered into a closed dry cleaner's parking lot.

"According to the tracker, he's parking at a pay-by-the-hour lot," Gage said.

Yep. He was switching vehicles. So he wasn't a complete idiot.

"He's getting into a Chevy Malibu. Dark green," Brooks said a few minutes later. "I'll tail him for three blocks, then turn off."

"We'll pick it up from there."

"You guys want me to take a turn following him?" Gage asked.

"No. Focus on finding out who he is."

"Affirmative."

Gage was trained, but finding out who this guy was would be a lot more important for the team. Because it would be one more way to figure out who the hell had hired these kidnappers in the first place. Then cut the head off the snake.

As Skye and Colt traded off with Brooks tailing the guy, Gage's familiar laugh made something ease inside Skye. Whenever he started laughing like a cartoon villain, she knew he'd hit gold.

"Got him. He's Steve Barclay. Thirty-five. Army vet. Married once. Divorced. No kids. And...he's got a federal warrant out for his arrest. For a long list of shit. Once we've got him locked down and get what we need, I say we call Hazel and do her a favor."

Hazel Blake was an FBI friend of Leighton's who had done them a solid not too long ago. Skye really liked the woman even if she was a Fed. "Agreed." Because doing favors for someone at a federal agency? Oh yeah. They might already have a couple "get out of jail free" cards in the form of some very interesting information they'd gathered during an op, but it never hurt to keep current contacts happy. She figured this was the version of normal people networking.

Barclay took them on a merry chase around Redemption Harbor, but since they were working as a team it was unlikely he'd seen their tail. If he had, he still led them back to a quiet suburban neighborhood where he parked at the last house on a cul-de-sac.

"It's a rental," Gage said once they gave him the address and he did his computer magic. The man really was a genius.

Made sense. Much easier to stay at a house as opposed to a hotel with nosy staff.

"From what I can tell there's a retention pond behind the house. Let's meet up on the other side and we'll move on the place. Take him quietly," Gage said. "I'm parking two blocks over at a gas station. No cameras."

Everyone murmured their version of affirmative.

* * *

"I'm taking point on this," Brooks said, his voice tight as if he thought they would argue with him.

The four of them had set up stations all around the rental house with Colt and Skye in the back near the retention pond. Gage and Brooks were in the front. They were all using the huge trees and neighboring houses for cover.

"Affirmative," Skye said even as Colt said the same.

"I've got him on a parabolic mic," Gage said. "Just a few movements and water running. Now it's off. Sounds like he took a quick shower."

"I say we wait half an hour and see if he rabbits out of here," Brooks said. "He saw that micro camera. If I were in the same position, I would have left too. Actually, I wouldn't have come back to my base at all."

"Yeah," Skye said slowly. "I wouldn't have either."

"Unless this is some sort of trap." Brooks added.

"Could be, but this guy isn't big-time." Gage's voice was as quiet as the rest of them. "He's competent, takes a few jobs a year, gets paid and lies low."

"Then we wait," Brooks said. "We're not losing anyone because we got impatient."

Out of all of them, Brooks was a pro at being patient. As a former sniper, he would have to be. She, on the other hand, hated downtime, and though she had been very good at what she did when she'd been a spy, the downtime had always made her stir-crazy. Still did.

"So what do you guys think of the name C-4 for the dog?" she murmured, scanning the house for any movement.

Brooks snickered across the line. "I think it sounds like something you would do."

"I can't believe we're getting such a small mutt," Colt muttered. "We should get a German Shepherd or something..."

"Something what? More manly? Please."

"I don't know, something bigger. Like a guard dog."

"I like C-4." She'd never had a pet before and the cute little Shih Tzu had the biggest, sweetest eyes. She'd have to be a monster to have turned the puppy down. "I see movement," Skye murmured, shifting into fight mode. A shadow peeled itself off the back of the house, moving stealthily toward the chain-link fence around the retention pond. Right toward where Colt was hiding.

"I got him." Colt's voice was whisper quiet.

He was closer to the moving figure. Still, Skye always got a little nervous whenever her husband put himself in danger. She figured that would never change, no matter how strong and capable he was. There was always going to be a part of her that simply worried for him. Even if worrying didn't do shit.

"We got your six." Brooks's response was just as quiet. Even though he'd wanted to take point on this, it didn't make sense when Colt had the best angle.

Skye remained where she was as Colt disappeared into the shadows, becoming nearly invisible as he used huge oak trees to his advantage. The moon was obscured by clouds tonight, giving them all an advantage. And there wasn't much light on the back side of this house and none illuminating the retention pond, which was definitely a bonus. The lack of light was probably the reason Steve the kidnapper had decided to exit out the back of the house. Maybe he knew he'd been followed or maybe he was simply taking extra precautions. She was betting on the latter, considering all the evasive driving he'd done. This guy thought he was safe, alone.

If there had been only one person following him, he would have lost the detail. But it was pretty damn hard to evade a team of drivers. It was one of the pros to working with a team. Something she appreciated now.

As he moved west, Skye remained in place, all the muscles in her body tense as she waited for the man to get close enough to where Colt was lying in wait. She couldn't even see Colt, but she knew where he had to be.

They'd all donned dark clothing and ski masks, because they were going to be turning this guy over to the Feds when they were done with him and they didn't want him to be able to identify them. The fewer people who knew who they were, the better. Even if this guy was a total douche, he might have a big mouth and someone might eventually listen to him if he talked about a team of people kidnapping him.

Like a jaguar bursting from the trees, Colt attacked with sharp precision, not making a sound as he body-slammed Barclay.

With a grunt, the man went down, and to give him credit he didn't panic. No, he started to fight, drawing his arm back for a punch.

But he was no match for Colt who had a hell of a lot of training, first with the Marines and then with the CIA.

Her husband moved swiftly, maneuvering the smaller man onto his stomach and gripping him in a chokehold as the guy clawed at the grass and dirt beneath them. Barclay flailed about, gasping as he fought the inevitable.

Skye raced toward the two of them even as she counted *one, two, three.* By the time she reached them, the man wasn't moving but Colt held firm, still putting pressure on his windpipe. Skye continued counting and when she reached the right number she said, "Stop."

Colt was already loosening his grip. Without pause, he'd grabbed the man's wrists and yanked them behind his back. Watching the way he moved, with such economic precision, it was hard not to admire how incredibly sexy he was as he hog-tied the man with a couple flex ties. Yep, that was her husband.

"I'll get the truck," she whispered, racing off into the darkness. It was time to get some answers.

CHAPTER SEVENTEEN

—Entitlement is a delusion built on self-centeredness
and laziness.—

Max slid his earpiece in as he steered into the parking lot of the local feed store. "Yeah?" he answered on the second ring. There was only one man who had this number. Well, not really a man, but a man-child. A moron, but Max wasn't picky about who hired him. The only thing he cared about was getting paid.

"Give me some news," Man-Child snapped.

This guy was impatient, but that was usually the way of it. Guys like this had to hire guys like Max because they were pussies and couldn't handle shit themselves. Max glanced around the parking lot to survey the other patrons. It was half full, which was good for him. He'd be leaving this vehicle here tomorrow after he'd wiped it down. "I'm in the process of getting to her. I should have her soon."

"I've heard that before." There was a tremor to the man's voice now. Probably because he was high. "And no one has delivered!"

"Well you should have hired me first." Max knew why the man-child hadn't, of course. He cost more. But Max was also better at his job. Mainly because nothing was ever personal to him. He viewed things with a critical eye and didn't make emotional decisions. Because the only thing that mattered to him was the bottom line. This kind of shit wasn't personal to the people he kidnapped or killed. They were just part of a business arrangement. Except this client was a pain in the ass. Everything for Man-Child was about emotions. Entitled moron.

Even going after this target was stupid. But it wasn't Max's problem. He'd do what needed to be done, drop her off to the client, and get his money.

"I'm not going to be available for communication for the next twelve hours, possibly twenty-four." Normally he didn't go into that much detail, but a client like this one needed his hand held. Max could adapt to the situation.

"Why?"

He held back a sigh. "Because I'm going to be doing my job. Taking her is going to be tricky now that she's gone to ground." And he was assuming she had since she wasn't at her place and her phone wasn't traceable. "I'll contact you when I'm in Miami." And not a moment before because that was not how he worked. He might hold this guy's hand a little, but he wasn't going to cater to him. He was doing a job and that was all that should matter to any client.

"Fine," the man snapped. "If you try to double-cross me—"

"You know my reputation." He cut the fool off. "I always get the job done." Of course there had been a few exceptions to that rule but the people he had decided to double-cross were all dead. So there was no one to ruin his pristine reputation. "Have you had contact with the others recently?" He needed to know if anyone else was going to get in his way. He'd simply eliminate anyone but he liked to know what he was up against.

"No. All three of them have gone radio silent."

That was interesting. This guy had gone off half-cocked because his pride was injured and he'd hired men without the correct skill set to kidnap someone. Not complete amateurs but not the best either. Not that Max was the absolute best either. He knew his limitations and only took jobs he thought he could do. Hadley Lane was a challenge only because of who her family was. He'd been getting a little bored, so he was actually looking forward to this job. "If you bring anyone else in to this job in the next forty-eight hours, I will hunt you down and kill you. And I won't be quick about it."

The other man cursed then said, "Understood."

The guy might be a fool but he wasn't completely stupid, Max thought as he ended the phone call. Then he took the battery out. He'd toss it out the window once he left here. First, however, he wanted to check out this feed store.

He'd figured out that the girl must be at her family's ranch. It was the most secure place and if he was hiding from someone, it was where he would choose to go. He hadn't been able to find out much about the brother other than he seemed to have a few business interests but mainly ran the Alexander Ranch. The girl hadn't posted anything on social media lately, so no leads there.

Her father, Douglas Alexander, was supposedly retired but still seemed to keep a finger in many of his businesses. And the man had just returned from Miami so Max's money was on him being at the ranch too. Maybe because he was concerned for his daughter? Who knew. The only thing Max knew was that if he wanted to grab the girl, he had to get on that ranch. Because all three of the men that had been hired to kidnap her were now missing or at least out of contact. That couldn't be a coincidence. So either Douglas Alexander had paid them off or he'd killed them. Which meant he might be waiting for a full-on attack.

Max was at the feed store because the Alexander Ranch got their deliveries weekly from it. And he was going to be on the next truck that made its delivery to them.

Sometimes the easiest way into any impenetrable fortress was the one that people tended not to pay attention to. Hired help often blended in. And he always used that fact to his advantage.

No one would expect this type of entry. And if he got this right, he'd get onto the ranch, get the girl, and get out. Of course, things rarely worked out so easily, but he wasn't afraid to do what was necessary to get a job done. And collateral damage was sometimes a reality.

CHAPTER EIGHTEEN

—Life is too short for bad sex and shitty people.—

Axel strolled around the perimeter of the Alexander estate, looking for any holes in the security. Since it was after dark, it would theoretically be easier for someone to hide. Though maybe not so much, because of the thermal capabilities of the security cameras. He'd already reviewed the exterior camera feeds but he wanted to see where they were positioned. C-4, potentially Skye's new dog, followed along with him, sniffing at everything but for the most part keeping up with Axel. She was a cute little thing, even if she was a mutt.

Once he'd done two sweeps of the estate, he knew it was time to go back inside. Even if he didn't want to admit out loud that he was avoiding Hadley, he knew that was exactly what he was doing. Because the whole declaration he'd made about waiting to have sex felt pretty stupid right about now. He was trying to protect himself, he could admit it. At least to himself. But he also knew that no matter what he did, if she walked away from him, he was screwed regardless. Because he'd already fallen for her. There was no turning back at this point for him. It didn't matter whether they'd had sex or not. And she was an adult. She said she wasn't going to regret him. He had to trust that.

And he really, really wanted to be inside her right about now.

When he stepped inside the back door, a blast of warmth hit him. He was surprised to find her sitting there at the kitchen island, sipping on a glass of red wine.

Her entire face lit up with a smile when she saw him, revealing that little dimple that drove him crazy. "Did C-4 take longer than you expected?"

He pulled his gloves off then shrugged out of his coat and hooked it on the coat rack by the door. "I was actually checking out the security cameras. Your dad let me look at all the security feeds but I still wanted to see where they were set up myself. He's got an incredible system here."

And apparently they had sensors all over the ranch so if someone inadvertently triggered them while sneaking around, an alert went out to Brooks, Douglas, and their security team.

"So listen," Axel said, feeling out of his depth. "I'm really into you." God, he felt like an idiot saying it like this. What the hell was he trying to say anyway?

It looked as if she was about to respond when her dad stepped into the kitchen.

Douglas Alexander gave a warm smile to Hadley and a civil, reserved one to Axel. "Hey sweetheart, I see you're taking advantage of the wine," he said, smiling.

She smiled at her dad. "It's the bottle you recommended and you are right, it's amazing."

"Would you mind if I steal your friend Axel for a few minutes? I wanted to talk to him about some security stuff."

Even Axel knew that was a big fat lie and he was pretty certain that Hadley did too but she simply smothered a smile and nodded. Then she picked up her glass of wine and winked at him. "You guys can use the kitchen, I'm headed to bed."

At the word *bed*, far too many images replayed in his mind and he had to shut them down fast. Especially since it seemed her dad was finally going to have some sort of talk with him. He'd been waiting for it. And he respected the guy for being concerned about his daughter. Axel knew that he was no prize. For the love of God, look at what he did for a living. If he had to prove himself, he would. He didn't care how long it took.

Once Hadley was gone, the older man stepped to the fridge. "Want a beer?"

He shook his head. He was going to be sober until this entire threat was neutralized. Not that he drank much anyway. "No, but thank you."

"So what did you think of the security around the house?"

"It's good. I'm impressed with the system you have and the layout. Nothing is ever flawless, but everything surrounding the house and the sensors you have set up, it's pretty damn close."

"And if anyone does breach the house, we are all armed. Not that it would be easy to find us without a fucking map of this place." Douglas laughed lightly.

Axel nodded, waiting for him to say something. When he didn't speak, Axel cleared his throat. "I care about your daughter. A lot. And I would never hurt her."

"I'm a pretty good judge of character. And I'm pretty sure you have absolutely no intention of hurting her. But if you do, I'll hurt you." Axel could respect that. No angry words or anything else, Douglas simply shook Axel's hand. "As long as you treat her right, you're okay with me."

"I will, sir. And fair warning, I'm serious about her. I'm not going anywhere."

The older man blinked, maybe at Axel's brusque tone.

And that was that—it was time to find Hadley. Ten minutes later, Axel wasn't panicked exactly, but he didn't like the heavy sensation that settled on his chest as he left Hadley's room—because she wasn't there.

The house was locked down and the security at the ranch was top of the line, but he'd assumed she'd be in her room. It didn't take him too long to make it back to his wing of the house. When he stepped inside his guest bedroom, he froze for a second.

Hadley sat on his bed, her laptop set up in her lap. She smiled when she saw him and closed it, putting it on the bedside table.

There was something so right about seeing her waiting for him in his bed. He wanted her there always.

"How did things go with my dad?" she asked, stretching out on the covers as if she belonged there.

"He just wanted to talk security."

She rolled her eyes. "He might have talked about security, but I guarantee he had something else to say to you."

Axel simply shrugged and locked the door behind him. He definitely didn't want to talk about her dad right now. "I hope you're planning to stay the rest of the night."

She lifted an eyebrow. "Maybe."

"Maybe?"

"Yeah, it depends on if you make it worth my while." The grin she gave him was a little bit sweet and a whole lot wicked. And even though she was fairly innocent, he knew there were a lot of layers to this woman. He wanted to spend a lifetime peeling all of them back.

Wordlessly, he stripped his sweater over his head as he stalked toward the bed.

Her breathing hitched slightly as she swept her dark gaze over his bare chest. He couldn't help the swell of pride at the hunger he saw there as she drank him in. He wanted her to like what she saw, to want him as much as he wanted her. Though that didn't feel possible.

There would be no more waiting between them. He didn't have enough self-control, not when she was offering herself up. There were so many things he wanted to say, had tried to say earlier, but failed.

Even if he wasn't good with words, he still needed to put himself out there. "I'm not experienced at relationships in general. But I want you to know where I stand. I want to move to Redemption Harbor—to be near you. I'll find a respectable job and be someone that you're proud of. I don't want to go back to my old life. And no matter what happens between us, I'm not going back to that." A solid truth. He'd been drowning for a long time in his own loneliness and meeting Hadley had been like seeing the light. Because that's what she was, a light in the darkness.

"That's a big change. To...give up everything." A little frown tugged at her kissable mouth.

He knelt on the edge of the bed, still not touching her because he wanted to get all of this out. "I'm not giving up *anything*. And hopefully I'm gaining you."

"You *have* me. We can worry about some of that future stuff later, but for now..." She reached for him.

That was all he needed as he moved onto the bed and on top of her. She had on matching pajamas with little dogs all over them. Which just made her more adorable. The top was a button-down so he took his time unhooking each button, his fingers grazing her soft, smooth skin. Every time he made contact, she shivered beneath him, watching him intently.

He'd never been nervous about sex before but he really didn't want to screw this up. Maybe that was part of the reason he'd been holding back. He never wanted to disappoint her, for her to question whether she'd made the right choice.

As she arched up, slipping her top the rest of the way off, he dipped a head to one breast.

Moaning at his kisses, she reached for the button of his jeans. "Are you sure about this?" Her voice was raspy and unsteady as she pulled his zipper down.

Her question surprised him, mainly because she was so sweet and sincere about it.

Pulling back, he cupped her cheek with one hand, stroking over her soft skin with his thumb. He knew without a doubt that he would never get tired of this woman. She was everything he never knew he'd been missing. "I feel like I should be asking you that question."

There went that wicked smile again. "I'm definitely ready."

The eagerness in her tone nearly undid him. That was all he needed to hear as he reached for the top of her pants and tugged them down her legs. No panties either. Holy hell, she was trying to give him a heart attack. He wondered if this was common for her or if she'd done it for him. He couldn't find his voice to ask her, however.

After tasting her last night, he was officially addicted. And it was the best kind of addiction.

Axel forced himself to go slow as he drank in all her soft curves and smooth, kissable skin. It was hard to think, let alone remember to breathe, as he knelt above her. Right about now he wished that he had four hands and two mouths. He wanted to kiss and touch her all over, to have her trembling from exhaustion with his name on her lips. He wanted her as addicted to him as he was to her.

For always.

"Pants off," she whispered.

Yeah, he could manage that. He'd been planning to keep them on as a small barrier but screw it. She was naked in his bed, wanting him.

There should be nothing between them anymore.

Hadley could tell that something had shifted for Axel, and while she wasn't sure what it was, she knew that it was a good thing. He didn't seem to be holding back anymore.

When he took his pants off, a pleasurable gasp escaped. She'd seen him before, had stroked him off, but seeing his thick length again… Oh yeah. The man was certainly blessed.

Her inner muscles tightened as she watched him crawl up her body and once again cover her, his mouth searching hers out. She arched into him, savoring the feel of her already sensitized nipples rubbing against his chest.

The man was hard all over. Scars nicked his chest and abs and she wanted to ask him about every single one. But later. Once she could think straight again.

Stroking her fingers down the tightly bunched muscles of his back, she only stopped once she reached his perfectly carved ass. When she dug her fingers in, he moaned into her mouth, the primal sound reverberating through her.

She desperately wanted to feel him stretching her, to come around his thickness. Yesterday had been like a little teaser before the real deal.

Reaching between their bodies, he cupped her mound, teasing a gentle finger along her folds. Knowing what he could do with his hands had her growing even slicker with need.

When he slid a finger inside her, she arched into him, wrapping her legs tighter around him. She felt as if they'd been building up to this from the moment they'd met. When he'd first smiled at her outside that coffee shop.

As he added another finger and began stroking so slowly she was certain he was trying to make her crazy, she bit his bottom lip.

He jerked against her, all his muscles pulling taut. So she did it again, nipping at him playfully. The sexy moans he made were worth everything.

Her inner walls tightened even more the faster he stroked and she knew it wouldn't take her long. "Not your fingers," she rasped out, glad he understood what she was trying to say. She wanted to come around him this time.

Leaning up, he looked down at her as he shifted position and poised his cock at her entrance. The way he watched her was as if he saw every thought inside her.

"Move." The word wasn't so much a demand as a plea.

Thankfully he thrust inside her, filling her completely and stealing her breath. As he started kissing her again, he cupped her face, his hold possessive. With his other hand he gently teased a nipple, rolling it with his thumb, slowly driving her crazy.

When she started rolling her hips, he met her stroke for stroke, the sensation of him filling her with pure bliss. All her inner muscles tightened harder and harder the faster he thrust inside her.

She ran her fingers over his back and chest even as he explored her body with his hands. Everywhere he touched her, her nerve endings flared to life. She wanted more, all of him.

Knowing he wanted to move to Redemption Harbor, to be near her...it was a lot to take. She should be freaked out. Instead, she loved the thought of being able to wake up with him, to do this every day.

When he started strumming her clit, that was all it took for her to find release. Her orgasm slammed into her hard and fast, overwhelming her as she arched up into him.

"Axel." She dug her fingers into his back as he thrust again, finding his own release.

He growled out her name as he buried his face against her neck, coming inside her in hard strokes until they collapsed against the bed, both breathing erratically.

She never wanted to leave the room, and while she wasn't remotely glad about the fact that someone wanted to kidnap her, she was grateful that this whole situation had brought Axel into her life.

Because she was pretty sure she wasn't letting him go.

CHAPTER NINETEEN

—You always have a choice.—

As she watched through the two-way mirror, Skye couldn't help but admire as her husband got ready to interrogate Steve Barclay, all-around douchebag.

She hated having to sit this one out, but she understood why she couldn't be the one to question Barclay. Once they were done with him they were going to basically giftwrap him for the Feds, and if he ever decided to talk about being questioned by some random guy who kidnapped him, it was better that it was a masked man. And not a woman. The three guys had done rock-paper-scissors and Colt had won.

Probably better, too, considering the guy had been planning to kidnap Brooks's sister. Even though the cowboy had wanted to take point, and he'd once been a stone-cold sniper, Barclay had still planned to kidnap his baby sister. Brooks had no business questioning the guy because he would likely lose his cool and Barclay would remember that later. They didn't want anything linking back to them.

"I want to be in there," Brooks growled.

Skye simply looked at him.

He lifted his shoulders. "I know it's good that I'm not in there. I'm just making a statement."

"So…I was thinking that instead of giving Barclay over to Hazel we should give him over to Agent Darius Moore. We can do it as an anonymous delivery."

Gage and Brooks were silent for a long moment, and Gage was the first one to speak. "Are you going to let him know the gift is from us?"

She snorted. "No, but if we ever need to call in a favor or if he ever figures out we were the ones to kidnap him in Miami, maybe this will give us some goodwill." They'd sort of kidnapped a DEA agent a few months ago. They'd only done it to save his life— and save Olivia and Savage's cover during an op. They'd been masked at the time and Skye was pretty sure that if Agent Moore dug hard enough he could figure out who they were. But he'd gotten credit for a huge bust because of them. The kind that made careers. Still, she felt a little bad about what they'd done, so giving him a present like this would ease her conscience.

Brooks shrugged. "I don't care who we give the guy to. But we do need to get Barclay out of my sight soon before I change my mind and kill him."

Skye wasn't sure if he was kidding or not so she simply nodded. Turning back to the two-way mirror, she adjusted the volume on the speakers so she could hear what was going on better.

She knew Colt didn't like to torture. No, he preferred psychological warfare. If she had to guess how Colt was going to play this, he'd end up threatening with torture in a subtle way. Back when they'd been in the CIA together, she'd watched him work and he was a master.

Barclay was now zip-tied to a chair and hooked up to a high-tech lie detector that synced with Colt's laptop.

"The machine doesn't lie, dumbass. Do you know who hired you, yes or no?" Colt's voice was deceptively casual.

"No. I already told you." He struggled once against the bindings.

It was clear the guy was lying from the spike on screen.

Colt shrugged, and shut his laptop. Then he lifted the small duffel bag he'd kept on the floor next to the table between him and Barclay. Casual as fuck, he unzipped it and pulled out a small rolled bag that reminded her of a makeup bag Mary Grace owned. When Colt popped the button and unrolled it to reveal a plethora of torture devices, the man strapped to the other seat shifted slightly, pulling at his bindings.

"I don't like torture," Colt said casually. "It'll get the job done, but you'll be in a lot of pain by the time I'm through and I'll have blood on my clothes. It's annoying."

The guy's eyes widened slightly as he shifted again, not so subtly struggling now as the chair scraped against the flooring. They'd bought this place months ago for this very reason—because Skye liked to be prepared—but it wasn't attached to their actual consulting building. On the outside, this place looked like a kept-up townhome, but they owned all of the attached townhomes as well. Under a bunch of shell corporations that would never trace back to the company. Because Gage was a genius.

"I don't know why you're bothering to protect the guy who hired you. Do you think he'd take torture for you? This is just a job, not top-secret bullshit. I seriously don't get why you're not talking right now." Colt lifted a shiny pair of pliers and inspected them under the light.

The guy cleared his throat. "How do I know you won't torture me after I tell you?"

Colt didn't stop inspecting his instruments as he said, "You don't. But I find torture to be a waste of time when you could simply tell me the truth. I don't care about you, I just want to know who hired you. I was hired by someone else, simple as that. How do you feel about losing your toes first? Or should I start with your fingers? I'm in a good mood so I'm going to let you pick. Usually guys go with the pinky toe first."

Skye snickered as the guy started panting, his breath becoming more and more labored. "Fine, I'll tell you! I'll tell you anything you want to know, man!"

Colt shifted the tools so that they were directly in front of the guy, right in his line of sight. Then he sat down and opened his laptop again. "For every lie you tell me, you lose a body part. If I ask if your favorite color is purple and you lie about it, there goes a toe. Nod if you understand."

Still breathing erratically, the guy nodded. "Yes, I understand."

"Good. Take a couple deep breaths, get yourself under control and I'll start with some basic questions."

And that was how it was done. Colt really was better at this than her. She'd have probably throat- or dick-punched Barclay by now. "We've definitely got him," she murmured. Next to her, Gage had his laptop open and was ready to start doing whatever sort of voodoo magic he did once he got the name of who'd hired Barclay.

And that was all they needed. A name. Once they had the guy who'd hired this loser, it would just be a matter of time until the threat was neutralized for good. Then Hadley would be safe.

* * *

Hadley sat at the center island in the kitchen with her dad and Axel—who was holding her hand as they listened to Brooks via speakerphone. Her dad had just woken both her and Axel even though it was three in the morning, so whatever was going on was important.

"Things are looking good," her brother said. "We just delivered the third man hired to kidnap Hadley to a federal agent. Anonymously. He was wanted on a pretty bad federal warrant. He never saw any of our faces so nothing should ever link to any of us. But Gage will be keeping an eye on him if he's ever released from prison."

Hadley squeezed Axel's hand once. That was definitely good news.

"Tell me you know who hired him," her dad said as he started the coffee maker.

"A man named Barron Fuller. I already know from Gage that you recently bought his business in a deal."

Her dad frowned. "Are you sure about that? I more or less bailed him out. He was ready to go bankrupt. I did him a favor—and bought the business at far greater than what it's valued at. And I only did it out of respect for his deceased father. Barron has a cocaine problem. And I don't know for certain, I still have accountants poring over the last few years, but I think he was skimming money. Probably to support his addiction. I...actually sat down with him, talked to him about his dad and tried to make sure he wasn't digging such a huge hole he couldn't get out of it."

"Well, Gage is sure. He started digging into the guy as soon as we got the name. Gage and I are headed to the ranch, and Skye and Colt are on their way to Miami as we speak. They're taking the jet."

"What are they doing down there?" Hadley asked.

"Taking care of the problem," Brooks said evasively. "I still want to keep you locked down at the ranch for now, until we know for certain that you're safe, but I think it's okay to say that you're out of the woods."

Relief flooded her system like a shot of adrenaline. She didn't know whether to laugh or cry. Hadley hadn't even realized the weight that had been sitting on her chest until it no longer existed. The man might not be in jail yet, but her brother and his team knew who the guy was. Which meant they would be able to stop him. "Thank you."

"You never have to thank me, little sister. Dad, will you take me off speaker? I need to talk to you."

As her dad picked the phone up, she turned to Axel and wrapped her arms around him as she buried her face against his chest. "I know it's not completely over, but it sure feels like it. I feel like I can breathe again."

He hugged her tight, resting his chin on top of her head as she inhaled his spicy scent. "As soon as this is officially over and you're free to leave, I'm taking you anywhere you want to go."

Smiling, she pulled back to look up at him. "Actually, the only place I want to go is to a rescue shelter. Even with my school schedule, I still have enough time for it and I really miss having a dog around the house." C-4 was adorable, but she was Skye's dog now and Hadley really wanted one of her own.

He laughed lightly. "Then it's a date."

She was almost afraid to feel any relief, and knew that things weren't settled yet but...she had hope. And her future seemed brighter than ever because of the very sexy man in her arms.

CHAPTER TWENTY

—Whatever doesn't kill me, better run.—

Skye leaned back in the plush leather seat of Brooks's private jet as she scanned her tablet. After dropping Barclay off to the DEA, they were making good time on their flight to Miami. "Man, this guy is crazy or stupid. Probably both," she said to Colt, referring to the man who'd hired contract killers to kidnap Hadley.

Barron Fuller III. A former frat boy with not only a cocaine problem, but a gambling one as well. He'd had everything given to him and amounted to nothing.

"Definitely crazy. Probably because of all the cocaine he's done," Colt muttered, scanning his own tablet.

"He should have been thanking Douglas for basically bailing him out. He bought the guy's company because of the respect he had for his father. Instead this guy took it as some weird slight against his pride. Or I'm guessing that's what this is. There's no way he would have been able to sell it for any more. And clearly he couldn't manage it."

The guy had been driving his business into the ground, skimming so much off the top that sooner rather than later, the IRS would have caught up with him. So what did the dumbass do? He took out a loan from a vicious, well-known loan shark in Miami. Gage had searched hard on this guy and the info he'd found was pure gold.

"I'm still not sure how we should deal with this guy," Skye said.

Colt nodded once in agreement.

They'd set Fuller up to meet with Barclay—who was now in custody of Agent Moore. In reality Fuller would be meeting with Colt, who was posing as Barclay. Since the two had never met in person, and Skye was going to be posing as an unconscious Hadley, it would be easy to fool the guy long enough to take him down. But they were also breaking some laws and didn't want to deal with a trial because there were so many loose ends. Like the fact that two of the hired hitters were dead and their bodies were missing. And the third was now in custody for an outstanding warrant. And there was no way Barclay was going to admit to being involved in this.

"It looks as if he has some outstanding debts with this loan shark," Colt said.

She let out a low whistle as she saw the number. "This guy really likes his cocaine."

"He's likely betting on getting money from Douglas in exchange for Hadley. Even though it seems pretty clear he never planned to turn her over anyway."

Barclay had admitted as much to them. And he hadn't cared either. He'd known that he'd be dropping the girl off with Fuller to be raped and tortured before being ransomed. And Barclay said he was pretty certain Fuller never planned to give her back. He was garbage too. She hoped he rotted in prison.

"If the loan shark is looking for him, we can just drop Fuller off on the guy's doorstep with a bow wrapped around his neck. Let him take care of the problem." Skye shrugged. It was a tactic they'd used before when they'd been with the CIA—and since starting Redemption Harbor Consulting. That way, they didn't have to clean up any messes and things basically took care of themselves without any involvement from them.

Her husband lifted a shoulder, his mouth kicking up in a grin. "I kind of like that idea. Then maybe we can spend a couple days in Miami before heading home. I wouldn't mind a few down days with my very sexy wife."

She smiled wickedly at him. "That sounds like a plan to me."

* * *

Skye was slumped over in the trunk of the car they'd rented, her wig covering most of her face as she feigned being unconscious. She'd done something similar before and though she hated remaining still, she could do anything for an op. And she could do just about anything right now because it would bring down an asshole and keep Hadley safe.

Forcing herself not to focus on the discomfort of lying on top of the spare tire, she listened as Colt talked to Fuller, who'd just arrived at the hangar to meet them. Now they simply needed to confirm that yes, Barron Fuller was behind everything.

It was pretty clear that he was, but before they tossed him to the wolves, they'd make sure.

"Did you hurt her?" A man's voice trailed closer.

"Nah." Colt. "Just knocked her out using a sedative. She might have gotten a little banged up in the trunk, but she's fine."

"You fuck her?"

"I don't touch the merchandise. Now where's my money?" Colt's voice was hard and nearby.

He'd be right at the open trunk now. There was a slight shuffling sound then the sound of a round being chambered. "You'll get paid when I get paid."

"That wasn't the deal," Colt snarled.

"Yeah, I know, but I'm changing things. I'm not double-crossing you!" The man sniffled. "I just gotta get my ransom and you'll get your money."

All right, it was time to "wake up." Skye whipped her SIG up as she rolled over and pointed it right at the guy's groin. "Drop your weapon and hands in the air!"

"You're a narc!" Former frat boy let out a squeal as he dropped the weapon he clearly had no business owning.

"Oh, you're going to wish we were cops by the time we're through with you." Colt's voice was silky smooth and quiet. A more terrifying sound than if he'd raised his voice.

Skye slid from the trunk and quickly surveyed the interior of the airplane hangar. They'd let the pilot go a while ago and told him they wouldn't need him for a couple more days. She was glad the guy hadn't returned unexpectedly because this might have been difficult to explain.

"You work for Douglas?" Fuller sniffled again, wiping his nose with the back of his hand. God, this guy was gross.

Colt motioned toward the ground. "Face down, hands behind your back. Don't make me ask again."

She loved it when he started giving out orders. Yeah, the timing was highly inappropriate but she couldn't help it that her husband turned her on. Always.

"Come on, who do you work for?" Fuller whined even as he complied. At least the drugs hadn't completely addled his brain.

Colt restrained Fuller's arms and legs and taped his mouth shut in less than thirty seconds. Seriously, could he get any hotter? Skye didn't think it was possible.

As Colt tossed the guy into the trunk, he leaned close to a wide-eyed, sniffling Fuller. "You're going to tell us everything we want to know or we're dropping you off at Jeremiah Dixon's place."

Fuller's eyes got wide at the mention of the brutal loan shark and he started trembling and attempting to shout against the tape even as Colt shut the trunk door.

"How long should we leave him in there?" she asked, striding over to the cooler where the pilot had left them a couple hoagies for an early lunch. She was starving.

"Twenty minutes should do it."

"You won't even need to threaten torture with this one."

"No shit."

Once they got what they needed from Fuller, they'd still deliver him to Dixon. Because this guy deserved it. Gage had done an even deeper search on Fuller and it turned out the guy had more than a drug and gambling problem. Seemed as if he didn't understand that no meant no. Yeah, Skye wouldn't be losing a moment of sleep for turning him over to another criminal.

CHAPTER TWENTY-ONE

—Being a sister is way better than being a princess.—

"What exactly did Skye and Colt say?" Hadley perched on the cushioned chair in Brooks's office since he'd asked her to meet him in here alone.

AKA without Axel.

He was really going to have to get over his dislike of the man because Hadley was pretty much over the moon for Axel. And she didn't think that was going to change anytime soon. Probably not ever. Which was sort of scary in and of itself but she'd worry about that later.

"They had a talk with the man who ordered your kidnapping and retrieved all of the information possible."

"Retrieved or extracted?"

Her brother simply grinned as he adjusted his cowboy hat. "Same difference."

"So you guys really just make your own rules, your own laws." The knowledge was a lot to take in.

He lifted a shoulder, clearly not apologetic. "I'm sorry if any of this makes you uncomfortable. We've all seen how shitty the legal system is, and honestly, I sleep fine doing what we do. I take care of my people."

She liked that last part a lot. "So...I'm okay to return to my life?"

"Fuller said he'd hired three men, all of whom match the descriptions of the men that Axel or we came in contact with. And Skye and Colt believe him."

"Is it normal that I'm still kind of afraid?"

"Yeah, of course. I would actually like it if you'd stay at the ranch through the rest of your spring break. We still want to make sure the threat is truly neutralized. And that way you and I can spend some time together."

She narrowed her eyes at his guileless expression. "That sounds really sweet, but what I'm hearing is that you want me to stay here and you're planning to kick Axel out."

He grinned again. "I didn't say it out loud—even if I was thinking it."

Hadley pushed up from her chair and placed her hands on Brooks's shoulders. Since he was leaning against the desk he was closer to her height though still a bit taller. "Look, you're my big brother and I get that there are rules or whatever that come with that. But I'm a grown woman and I like Axel. I know who he is and I'm okay with it. So I need you to be okay with him too. Because I really want to have an honest, grown-up relationship with my family. I dealt with enough manipulative garbage from my mom, and honestly I can't see either you or dad doing that, but I still want us to be open about everything. And yes, I would really like it if you were okay with my boyfriend."

Saying the word boyfriend felt kind of weird but she and Axel were exclusive so she guessed that was what they were. Right? She really needed to clarify that with him. Though the man had said he wanted to move to Redemption Harbor for her and give up his life as a hit man. So maybe she didn't need to clarify.

"Why did you have to go and be all logical?" Brooks laughingly pulled her into a hug and kissed the top of her head. "Fine, I will make a serious effort to like him. I already invited him to go out practice shooting with me and the guys."

When she and her girlfriends hung out, they liked to go shopping or watch movies and eat bad food together. "I don't even know what to say to that."

He slung an arm around her shoulders. "Come on, let's go find Darcy and Axel. Olivia, Savage, Valencia, Martina and Mercer and Mary Grace should be here in a couple hours. Oh, and the baby. And Darcy was talking about cooking a big feast for everyone."

"Darcy is cooking?" Hadley asked doubtfully.

Her brother barked out a laugh. "Exactly. That's why I want to see what they got up to. Let's see if we can convince her to get takeout instead."

By the time they made it to the kitchen, Darcy, Axel and Hadley's dad were standing around the island while her dad spoke in quiet tones to someone on the phone.

She knew something was wrong by the expression on his face. "What is it?" she asked the others.

He set his phone down before they could respond. "One of the horses got out and knocked down a fence. Impaled herself on it. I tried to get the vet out here but she's on another emergency. Her whole practice is on emergencies." Her dad raked a hand through his hair.

"I can help," she said, feeling sick for the poor horse. "I'm obviously not a vet, but I've watched enough surgeries and I might know what to do. It's at least worth a try. And I can reach out to my friend from school," she said, already moving toward the back door, her cell phone in hand. Her friend didn't answer so she shot off a quick text.

Her dad shoved his own phone into his pocket and nodded as he joined her. Axel was right behind him. When it was clear that Brooks was going to come too, she shook her head. "It's okay, you guys get stuff ready for dinner tonight. We got this."

She knew that if a horse had been injured, the less people involved the better. The animal wouldn't need or want a bunch of people around, crowding it in. She also knew there was no way Axel was leaving her side, something she was pleased about.

"What kind of medical supplies do you guys have on hand in the barn?" Hadley asked as she rode shotgun in the ATV across one of the fields. The dirt road was a little bumpy but fairly smooth given that it wasn't paved.

Her dad glanced behind him as they pulled up to the barn. "Axel, grab that bag back there."

Axel picked it up as they parked and her dad took it from his hands before giving it to her. "I'd planned to give this to you later today as an early birthday gift. I know you won't technically need it for a few years, but it's yours."

She took the custom-made, dark brown leather doctor's bag filled with instruments and supplies and when she peered inside she realized this had cost a lot of money. "Thank you so much," she said. She would thank her dad again later because this was incredible, but now they needed to get to that horse. "What's the horse's name?" she asked as they hurried toward the opening of the barn.

"Nelly. She's young, new to our stable, and not quite trained yet. She got spooked by something. The fence was sturdy though so I know it's not shoddy workmanship. She's just a strong thing."

Hadley heard the horse before they saw it and her dad's foreman stepped out of one of the stalls, his expression dark. "Did y'all get ahold of the vet?"

Her dad shook his head. "No, but I got the next best thing."

It warmed her heart that her dad had so much faith in her. She just hoped she could help. She'd watched so many surgeries over the years and she'd been lucky enough to shadow the vet she'd worked for before. But taking responsibility for an animal's life by herself was something else entirely.

Her dad squeezed her shoulder once. "You got this."

His confidence in her, even if it was based on nothing other than fatherly love, gave her the shot of self-assurance she needed as she headed toward the stall with her dad. It was time to get to work.

CHAPTER TWENTY-TWO

—The moment I met her, I knew I was
looking at my future.—

Hadley stepped out of the stall an hour later covered in grime, hay and a little blood. Still, she was so happy because she was fairly certain that Nelly was going to make it. The plank hadn't gone nearly as deep as they'd feared. It had penetrated her pec muscle but hadn't broken any ribs. She'd pulled the plank out and sewed her up, first the layer of muscle, then the skin. She'd seen the same injury before on different horses and was confident she'd done everything right. The vet would be here in an hour once her own emergency was over to check on the horse regardless. The foreman had already left so he could meet her at the front gate. Because of the security restrictions in place right now the vet was going to be escorted onto this part of the property.

"You did a great job," her dad said, pulling her into a hug. "I'm going to go grab you some water," he said, stepping back and heading for the exit. She knew there was a cooler in the ATV and even though the water wouldn't be cold she didn't care. As long as it was wet.

"You can go with him," she said to Axel. "I just need a minute alone to decompress."

He frowned, but nodded and she was glad he didn't push. The emotional toll of seeing an animal in pain was always draining. There was no way around it for her. Her former boss and mentor had warned her that getting into this profession wasn't for the faint of heart and she'd been right.

It was usually the worst when an animal had been injured intentionally by a human, whether it was their owner or not. But days like this still sucked too. There was no bad guy in this scenario, just an injured horse in a lot of pain and afraid. The fear from the animals was awful because she wanted to take all of it away.

Running a hand over her face, she leaned back against a neighboring stall and simply took a deep breath. In and out. It helped to calm the riot of emotions inside her. Once she felt ready, she headed outside into the bright sunlight—and froze when she saw a man holding a gun on her father and Axel.

"Get in the ATV or I kill your father." The man's voice was neutral, but ice cold. He had on a mask which made him even creepier. But it also meant that he might let her father and Axel live.

Both men looked beyond pissed, like caged tigers ready to pounce. Their phones were on the ground next to them, smashed to bits.

She was numb as she stared at the man with the gun. Getting into that ATV with this masked man would certainly mean death for her, but...she had to do it. She couldn't risk him shooting her father or Axel. She simply couldn't allow it.

"Now. Or I'll start with his knees." He gestured the gun at her father. "It's a painful way to die."

Axel's face tightened. "Don't—"

The man cut Axel off and fired a shot into the ground. She nearly jumped a foot, her heart rate kicking up a thousand beats a minute. Because of the suppressor on the weapon, the sound didn't carry. But it was all the motivation she needed. Still clutching her bag as if it was a lifeline she started for the ATV, her movements stiff. She didn't look at her father or Axel because if she did, she'd break down.

She was supposed to have been safe. Everything was supposed to have been over. But it wasn't. This man was somehow here on her father's secure property. Holding a gun on two people she loved.

Heart racing out of control, she forced her legs to obey her as she slid into the passenger seat. As she sat, she slipped a small scalpel out of her bag before dropping the bag to the floor at her feet.

"No. You're gonna drive." Ice coated the masked man's words as he moved toward the vehicle. "And if you try anything, I'll shoot you. Contract only says you have to be alive."

Instead of getting out again, she just slid over into the driver's seat. Her palms were sweaty despite the chill in the air. And her chest hurt with each breath she dragged in as she fought the panic swelling inside her.

"The guy who hired you, Fuller, he's dead." Her dad's voice was dark, angry, a tone she'd never heard from him before.

The man with the mask paused once as he moved toward the ATV, though his gun hand never wavered. "If that ends up being true, I'll ransom her back to you."

"I'll pay you double what Fuller offered you. Just let her go."

"You'll pay quadruple." The man grinned once, his white teeth and lips visible even with the mask. His smile was like a shark. "Even if Fuller's not dead, I'll be in touch. Get your money ready, old man."

As he slid into the passenger seat, she glared at him. "You'll never get away with this. Even if you kill me, they'll hunt you to the ends of the earth." Something she intrinsically knew to be true.

She saw the hand coming, knew he planned to backhand her either for her words or to send a message to her father and Axel. This was her only chance. She lashed out with the scalpel, stabbing at his leg and aiming for the femoral artery.

The man screamed in pain as his hand went wild, grazing her forehead instead of her face. From there, everything was a blur of motion.

Axel moved faster than should be humanly possible, attacking the man like an animal. His fist connected with the man's jaw before he dragged him out of the passenger seat. The gun fell to the floorboard so she scooped it up even if she had no idea how to use it.

Her dad was suddenly there, taking it from her hands as Axel pounded his fists into the man's face. Over and over, the guy's head slammed into the hard earth beneath them.

"Axel." She didn't scream or raise her voice but somehow he must have heard her. He stopped, his hand around the throat of the now unconscious man. "Please don't kill him," she whispered. She didn't want him to have any more scars on his soul or for him to go to jail. Even if this guy probably deserved it, she simply couldn't stand the thought of Axel being the one to end his life.

"Take her back to the main house, *now*," her dad ordered Axel, tucking the gun in the back of his pants. "Do it." A not so subtle order.

"Dad—"

"No. Go with Axel." He gave Axel a hard look without even glancing at her.

"But—"

Without a word Axel took her by the elbow and scooped her up even though she could walk just fine. Gently, he set her in the passenger seat. When he cautiously took the bloody scalpel from her tight grip she belatedly realized she was still holding on to the thing. Then he brushed his lips over her forehead once.

She wanted to ask what her dad was going to do or if they were going to call the cops but she wasn't sure she wanted the answer. Her new reality... She wasn't certain if it was something she could live with. She'd always viewed the world, if not in black and white, as at least governed by certain rules and laws.

Now everything she knew had been turned upside down. And it scared her how easily she'd accepted everything.

Neither of them spoke on the way back to the ranch. After he parked, he strode around to her side and carried her, ignoring her feeble protest. When they reached the back door leading to the kitchen she finally said, "I'm okay to walk." At least she hoped she would be. She felt a little shocky.

His jaw tightened once, but then he nodded and set her on her feet as if she was made of porcelain. When they strode into the kitchen and found not just Darcy and Brooks there, but all the others, including sweet six-year-old Valencia, she just about collapsed. God, what if that maniac had made it to the house? What if— *Nope.* She couldn't deal with those thoughts now. Not when she was barely keeping it together.

She realized that Axel had said something to push the others into action as Brooks and Savage bolted out the door but she couldn't actually remember what he'd said. Could barely focus on anything as her trembling got worse. She could have died a few minutes ago. Her father could have died. Axel could have died.

He was now saying something to her. Looking up into his blue eyes, she forced herself to focus on him, on his mouth. It was pointless because she didn't comprehend anything. Jaw tight, he shook his head and scooped her up into his arms again.

Minutes later they were in her bathroom as he stripped off her grimy clothes. Blood was on her fingers and she wondered if it was from the horse or from the man. When Axel guided her into the hot shower, for a moment she thought he was going to leave her and almost panicked.

Then he stripped and dumped his own clothes into the pile with hers. Standing under the hot jets, he pulled her into his arms.

"I'm sorry," Axel murmured, his voice slightly muffled against the top of her head.

"You have nothing to be sorry for."

"I was going to kill him right there in front of you. I...I'm sorry."

She tightened her grip around his naked body. "If you had, it would have been okay." Even as she said the words she knew they were true. She didn't ever want him to think she judged him. If they went into this relationship with him worried that she held something over his head or had moral superiority or whatever...just no. He'd made choices and he was living with them. Not ones she could ever make, but...she loved him.

"Hadley—"

She pulled back to look up at him. "I feel like a mess right now. A hot, flaming mess of emotions. I'm living in a new reality where my family doesn't call the cops when there's a kidnapping contract on me. One where the man I love used to kill people for a living. One—"

His eyes went intense. "You love me?"

"Yes?"

"Is that a question?"

"Yes. I mean no. I...do love you." And now she felt a billion times more vulnerable, standing naked in front of him as she admitted it.

"Thank God. I love you too."

Her heart turned upside down, relief rushing through her. "Really?"

"I think I fell a little in love with you when you spilled coffee on me."

She smiled even as tension coiled tight in her belly. "I don't know if I'm cut out for all this. For these shades of gray. For what...I'm pretty sure is happening to that guy right now."

His gaze was steady on hers. "Do you want to involve the cops?"

"Would you be okay with that?"

"Whatever you need to happen, I'll make happen." The truth was in his gaze.

She shook her head. "No. It...can't happen. I understand that on every level. I just... I don't know. I think it's going to take time for me to process all the changes in my life."

He stroked a big hand up and down her back. "I'll give you as much time as you need."

"Wait…I don't mean without you." She tightened her grip around his waist, afraid he'd bolt.

"Really?"

"Yeah, really. I'm just giving you warning that it's going to take time for me to process everything, that's all."

"You can take all the time you need. I'm not planning on going anywhere." He kissed her then, his lips soft at first before morphing into a hard, possessive kiss that sent spirals of awareness throughout her entire body.

Yeah, whatever it was she had to do to deal with her new reality, as long as Axel was by her side, things would work out. She knew that without a doubt.

* * *

Axel's gaze strayed over to where Hadley sat with Mary Grace and Olivia as the three of them listened to whatever the animated Valencia was telling them. The little girl was completely unaware of what had happened earlier in the day.

Thank God for that.

When he realized Brooks had said something to him, he jerked his attention back to the man and Douglas. "What?"

Brooks just shook his head. "I said you're welcome to stay here for the next week with Hadley—because she's not going anywhere." He said the last part like a challenge, as if Axel might argue.

"Thank you." It wasn't like the other man could keep Axel from Hadley but he figured that responding civilly was the best way to go. "Did you ever figure out how he got on the property?" Axel asked quietly.

Douglas nodded, his expression dark. "Stowed away on the bottom of the feed delivery truck. I've shored up that security hole. We'll be doing more thorough inspections on all vehicles that enter the property."

"Good." The hitter who'd made it onto Douglas's property wouldn't be a problem to anyone anymore. Axel didn't know where they'd taken the body and he didn't care. He only cared that Hadley was safe. She hadn't asked any more questions about what had happened to the guy and he figured she might not ever ask. She might not want to know the truth.

"How's my daughter doing with everything?" Douglas asked.

"She's handling it. I think it'll be difficult for her at first. She's always lived by a set of rules, and this past week..." He lifted a shoulder as his gaze strayed back to her. "She's resilient."

"At least we know the threat is finally over," Brooks said.

"You're sure?" Because he'd thought only three men had been hired. Not four.

"Yeah. Gage followed Fuller's communication and money trails and it looks as if he was only in contact with this last guy once he lost communication with the first three men he hired. And now that Fuller's dead..." Brooks shrugged.

Axel frowned. "You're sure?"

Brooks pulled his phone out of his pocket, typed in his code and handed it over. Axel read the headline for the Miami Herald article. *Deceased Magnate's Son Dies of Apparent Overdose.* He scanned the article before handing it back to the cowboy.

"I'm surprised he wasn't found shot or tortured to death." The loan shark he'd owed money to was purportedly vicious.

"Apparently Dixon is being watched by the police, and with Fuller's loose relationship to him, maybe he didn't want the extra heat so he faked the overdose. Or maybe Fuller really did overdose."

Doubtful, considering the guy had been dropped off to Dixon. But Axel didn't care how the guy had died. Just that he was no longer an issue to the woman he loved. "I've started looking at places in Redemption Harbor," he said abruptly. "I'll make sure the place I buy has proper security and that Hadley is taken care of. So you better deal with it." He looked at Brooks as he said the last part because Douglas actually seemed all right with him.

Brooks simply returned the hard stare before holding out his hand. "Welcome to the family."

Blinking once, he took the other man's hand and pumped once.

Surprising him even more, Brooks continued. "Since you're going to need a new job, how do you feel about working with our team?"

He blinked again. "I like the sound of that."

"Good. We'll talk more later. Go see Hadley."

Brooks didn't need to tell him twice. It had taken all Axel's willpower to be separated from Hadley for the last ten minutes, and only because she was within his line of sight. After seeing her with a weapon to her head like that... Hell, he wasn't sure he'd get over that anytime soon. Or ever.

She looked over at him as he approached and the smile she gave him was blinding. He really wasn't certain what he'd done to deserve her, but he was never, ever letting her go.

EPILOGUE

—Be the person your dog thinks you are.—

Five months later

Hadley smiled at the sound of little puppy paws running across the wood floor as she stepped into the house she now lived in with Axel. They were in a gated community and Axel had gone a teeny bit overboard with the security. Not that she blamed him, and after what she'd been through, she was more than okay with some extra security measures.

It sure helped her sleep easier at night. Well, that and the sexy, capable man who warmed her bed on the nights he was in town helped too.

As she hung her backpack on the hook in the laundry room, she grinned as Lucky scratched the door separating him and her. She threw it open and crouched down to be inundated with kisses all over her face. The German Shepherd was afraid of his own shadow and acted as if he hadn't seen her for eight years when in reality it had been a mere two hours.

Seriously, this was the best way to be greeted every day. By the time she was done with cuddle and kiss time, she was ready for a glass of wine and food. Her class this afternoon had been good, but long. And she had a bunch of homework to start on tonight too. And before all that she needed to take Lucky out for a walk.

As she stepped fully into the kitchen she froze to see Axel standing next to the island, a grin on his face. She launched herself at him, throwing her arms around his neck as she tackled him. "I didn't think you'd be home until tomorrow!"

He caught her to him, hugged her hard. "Job ended early… I wanted to see how long you were going to cuddle with Lucky. I swear he gets more love than me," Axel mock grumbled as Lucky sat next to the two of them, whining.

"You're so full of it," she murmured, brushing her lips over his. "I missed you."

"I missed you too." He kissed her again, harder this time, only pulling back when Lucky nudged his entire body between the two of them.

Laughing, she crouched down and rubbed his ears. "I don't know if he's jealous of you or me."

Axel just snorted and went for the treat container. "I'm pretty certain he's jealous of me—because you're his favorite."

She shrugged as Axel pulled out a bone for Lucky to gnaw on. "He does have good taste."

"How was school today?"

"Good. Long, but good." It had taken Axel a while to be okay with her going to school after the whole kidnapping contract. But she couldn't live her life in a bubble, something they both knew. At least she was more aware of her surroundings now and always carried pepper spray—and Skye had been teaching her self-defense. Or more accurately, ways to completely incapacitate people so that they were writhing puddles of pain.

"I was thinking of ordering takeout. Will you grab the menu for me?" he asked as he pulled a bottle of her favorite champagne from the fridge.

Ooh, champagne sounded like heaven. She pulled out the menu from their favorite restaurant and when she turned to face him—found him down on one knee with Lucky posed next to him, his tail wagging wildly. A little box was in Lucky's mouth. Axel gently took it from him and opened it up, his hands actually trembling as he did.

"Will you marry me?"

Throat tight with too many emotions, she nodded as he slipped the ring on her finger.

"I'm going to need an audible answer." His tone was oh so serious.

"Yes," she rasped out. "Yes, yes, yes! And I don't want to do a long engagement."

Grinning, he stood and pulled her into his arms, kissing her so thoroughly that pleasure curled out to all her nerve endings. Finally he pulled back. "I love you, Hadley. I knew my life changed the moment I met you, I just had no idea how much."

She felt exactly the same. Her entire world had shifted on its axis the moment Axel O'Sullivan had walked into her life.

Her life had never been so full. She had a huge, often overprotective family—blood-related and otherwise—and now she was going to marry the man who'd brought so much color into her world. Even a year ago she couldn't have imagined this would be her life. Now, she couldn't imagine it any other way.

Thank you for reading INNOCENT TARGET, the latest book in the Redemption Harbor series. If you don't want to miss any future releases, please feel free to join my newsletter. Find the signup link on my website:

http://www.katiereus.com

ACKNOWLEDGMENTS

It's time to thank my usual crew! Kari Walker, thank you a thousand times over for all that you do! Sarah, thank you for all the behind the scenes stuff you do so I can write. I'm also grateful to Julia for her wonderful editing and to Jaycee for another gorgeous cover. For my readers, you all are the best! Thank you again for embracing this series. As always, I'm incredibly thankful I have such a supportive family. Last, but not least, I'm thankful to God for everything.

COMPLETE BOOKLIST

Red Stone Security Series
No One to Trust
Danger Next Door
Fatal Deception
Miami, Mistletoe & Murder
His to Protect
Breaking Her Rules
Protecting His Witness
Sinful Seduction
Under His Protection
Deadly Fallout
Sworn to Protect
Secret Obsession
Love Thy Enemy
Dangerous Protector
Lethal Game

Redemption Harbor Series
Resurrection
Savage Rising
Dangerous Witness
Innocent Target
Hunting Danger

The Serafina: Sin City Series
First Surrender
Sensual Surrender
Sweetest Surrender
Dangerous Surrender

Moon Shifter Series
Alpha Instinct
Lover's Instinct
Primal Possession
Mating Instinct
His Untamed Desire
Avenger's Heat
Hunter Reborn
Protective Instinct
Dark Protector
A Mate for Christmas

Darkness Series
Darkness Awakened
Taste of Darkness
Beyond the Darkness
Hunted by Darkness
Into the Darkness
Saved by Darkness
Guardian of Darkness

ABOUT THE AUTHOR

Katie Reus is the *New York Times* and *USA Today* bestselling author of the Red Stone Security series, the Darkness series and the Deadly Ops series. She fell in love with romance at a young age thanks to books she pilfered from her mom's stash. Years later she loves reading romance almost as much as she loves writing it.

However, she didn't always know she wanted to be a writer. After changing majors many times, she finally graduated summa cum laude with a degree in psychology. Not long after that she discovered a new love. Writing. She now spends her days writing dark paranormal romance and sexy romantic suspense.

For more information on Katie please visit her website: www.katiereus.com. Also find her on twitter @katiereus or visit her on facebook at: www.facebook.com/katiereusauthor.

Made in the USA
Coppell, TX
24 August 2020

34708184R00135